WITH VISIONS OF RED

BROKEN BONDS: BOOK THREE

TRISHA WOLFE

LOCK KEY PRESS

" Whoever fights monsters should see to it that in the process he does not become a monster. When you gaze long enough into the abyss, the abyss gazes back into you.

— **FRIEDRICH NIETZSCHE**

TWO YEARS AGO

SADIE

The crunch of gravel beneath my heels echos against the tall pines shrouding the out-of-the-way bar. A solitary lamppost illuminates the seedy little building, shining a spotlight right on my target, as the softly muffled twang of country music from within beckons me closer.

I smooth my palms along my hips and suck in a steadying breath, feeling exposed. The skimpy red dress leaves nothing to the imagination—and no hiding place for my gun. Not that I would dare bring it. This circumstance requires caution, but also common sense. Still, the missing steel against my hip leaves me feeling more than vulnerable.

Exactly how he likes them.

A loud burst of laugher greets me as I pull the wooden door open, and a gust of cigarette smoke blasts my face. The smoky plumes waft and curl in the dim lighting of the green plastic lamplights. The smell makes my back teeth clench, the craving hitting me hard. I bite the inside of my cheek, wishing I'd bought a packet of gum. I push through, my gaze sweeping over the strangers seated at the bar top, standing around the five pool tables, and the one man stationed at a lone corner table.

He's only slightly less out of place than I am in this establishment. Dressed in black slacks and a white button-up, his dark hair mussed after a long day, he's miles away from the city in which he works. He could change his clothes before he makes his daily trek to the outskirts of Roanoke, but he likes the attention he receives from the girls. He's not overdressed—just the right touch of sophisticated finery to denote he has a bit of money. Not enough attention to cause a ripple with the truckers; more of an air about him that states he likes to unwind from a hectic day with them. He's really one of them. *Accept me.* And for the girls…he's handsome enough. Reserved. Stoic. Polite. Even bashful at times. It's not his first rodeo, but every time is like the first for him. He never gets used to it.

And they love that. Because he treats them better than any truck driver passing through, looking for a quick, drunken screw. He promises them a reprieve; an easy and maybe even enjoyable romp. I can see the girls at the bar

2

now, fingering their hair-sprayed, teased layers, inching their jean skirts higher, batting their mascara-coated lashes his way.

He doesn't even have to try.

That's his farce.

Shaking my hair off my shoulders, I brazenly head for a table near the back wall. I can feel eyes on me, checking me out, hungrily roaming every inch of exposed skin— except for my chest. The dress stealthily designed to display my curves and flesh, while concealing that one, particular area with a choker-style collar that vees down around my breasts.

I battled some on whether I should leave my neck bare or not. It's his fascination with the neckline that ultimately decides *who*. I wasn't confident that mine would tempt him enough…and so better to leave it to the full imagination. Sometimes it's what you *don't* see that drives you crazy. Stirs the monster within to act.

Besides, I've been dying to wear this dress for him. The tight, silky fabric clings to my thighs as I saunter past his table. We both like to keep our backs to the wall, our vision unobstructed—a safeguard strategy for predators and prey alike. I can't discern him watching, but I can feel his awareness of me, his arousal. I've studied his tastes. I've learned his triggers. I've applied them and enhanced myself to fit his selection process. And I'm wearing his favorite color.

Another thing we have in common.

In a dank and colorless room, I'm the brightest object —the one to capture your gaze and ensnare you. And that's the mission. Become the bait, set the trap, and lure the hunter into his own web.

I've been coming to this bar on and off for the month that I've been stationed in Roanoke, and I've been here almost every night for the past week. I followed him here the first time. Watched him watching the girls. He chooses sex workers because they're easy to make disappear with little consequence. Though I've since learned he has much finer tastes—rich, powerful, domineering women—he's disciplined enough to play it safe. That's why I know he won't be able to resist me.

I'm not just a working girl; I'm a wealthy, high-class call girl. An escort. I'm a bit risky for him, because I might be missed. I have a select clientele that probably includes members of law enforcement—but I'm also just too tempting. I'm counting on his need overriding his self-control. He *needs* to assert his power over me. Dominate me. Show me just how wrong I am for flaunting my audacious self on his turf.

I just have to make sure I keep his attention, and that means eliminating the competition.

As I take my seat at the table, a middle-age waitress walks up and crosses her arms over her ample chest. "Sweetie, I don't know what game you're playing, but none of the boys here are taking the bait."

For an alarming second, icy pinpricks needle my chest. The fear of being made clogs my throat. "Excuse me?"

She pops her gum between her teeth. "Mostly truckers and a few lowlife locals. That's all we have here. What you're selling is too rich for their blood." She scans her eyes over my silk dress. "And you're pissing off the regulars." She nods to a couple of working girls at the bar. "Why don't you find a nice joint in the city to work?"

I catch the gaze of one of the sex workers and earn a nasty sneer. *You're welcome.*

Lifting a shoulder, I shrug. "I'm stuck here until I get my car out of the shop. It broke down. I'm just passing through."

She smiles. "Well, if you want some advice—" she uncrosses her arms and pulls a pencil from her coiffed hair "—tone it down some, honey. You're scaring the boys. They like to keep it simple. That means the price is right, ya know? Can I get you your regular?" At my nod, she winks and heads off to pour my drink.

As long as I'm here intimidating the locals, he's not hunting them. But the waitress does have a point: I stand out too much. I wanted to entice him...not disrupt his routine. And I'm running out of time to catch him.

Detective Quinn—the uptight asshat I've been assigned to assist twice now—has shut down the profile. He really doesn't like working with a behaviorist—with *me*. We've butted heads the whole time I've been in Roanoke. I swear he's from some ancient time before behavioral science. Like my skills are about as useful to him as a crystal ball. And he treats me like a green rookie who never clocked one single hour in the field. Like a delicate but irritating pain that cramps his hard-boiled detective style.

I'm not breakable. I'm not delicate.

And if he'd just apply the profile to the case, he'd see what I do: the man sitting adjacent from me. Mid-thirties. Attractive. Charismatic. With an inside knowledge of forensics, and a hatred for strong women that makes him impotent in real life situations.

But Quinn is stubborn. Too damn stubborn to put the heat on Lyle Connelly, because Connelly has an alibi for the most recent murder, and because the forensic tech works within the local department. The fact that this recent murder happened within a month of the last denotes the offender is escalating. He's been astonishingly patient in the past, waiting almost a year between attacks to claim his victims. The sudden detour in MO is what brought us here.

While Quinn and his task force focus on the recent vic, tracking leads in Roanoke, I've been examining the pattern. Putting together the profile. The biggest aspect of which points to someone in law enforcement—someone with knowledge of forensics; who avoids praise but demands promotions and recognition from higher-ups. A classic narcissist.

But that's not what sealed Connelly as the Roanoke Roper for me; it's the trail of brutally murdered women he's left throughout Virginia. He was present in each city when a murder was reported. But here's the kicker: his method changes from place to place, as if he creates a new MO each time. Honestly, it's a brilliant tactic. One that takes extreme discipline for a ritualistic offender.

Over the past three years, I've worked many of the cases, all unsolved—until now. It all keeps coming back to Connelly.

I finally found him.

Quinn, however, refuses to dig further to unearth the truth. Like Quinn, I don't want to ruin a reputation. I don't want to embarrass either of our departments. But isn't that the price we have to pay, the sacrifices we have to make, to bring in these offenders?

By the book, Bonds. We work within the law. We're not vigilantes.

Maybe Quinn is right; I am green, with a youthful idealism of the law to boot. I've been witness to the dark underbelly of the world. I've seen these creatures up close, smelled their breath, tasted their thrill, gazed into the blackness of their soulless eyes. I've been seared and branded by their cruelty. My body and mind violated by their evil.

Quinn believes he's sheltering me from this dark realm. By dismissing my theories and trying to get me thrown off his case, he's offering me some kind of backhanded protection. But if he had a bit more training in *my* field, he might see that I'm way past that point—the

7

moment to shelter me died in a dungeon. And in this dark world of ghouls and demons, I'm the monster to be feared.

All his old-school chivalry aside, Quinn strikes a cord in me—a deep one. Despite his anal, by-the-book shit, I do respect him. That's why I'm out here now, gathering intel on Connelly. I don't feel the need to prove myself or my theories, or to justify myself—but I'll be damned if this predator kills another woman right under my watch.

I'm pulled out of my thoughts as the waitress returns with my champagne. "Don't get a lot of requests for this," she says as she sets the flute before me. "Had to order it in special just for you."

"Thanks." I take a sip, my lips puckering at the tartness of the cheap champagne. "What's his drink?" I nod toward Connelly.

"Him? Mr. Lonely Hearts. SoCo on the rocks."

"I'll have one also," I say, receiving a raised eyebrow from the waitress.

"It's your liver, darlin'."

As she sets off, I push back in the chair and uncross my legs slowly, piquing the interest of several men around the nearest pool table. Connelly remains unaffected. His head is bowed over his tumbler, as if he's studying the grains in the wood table.

When the waitress places the glass of SoCo in front of me, I note his slight shift in posture. His shoulders twitch upward, his neck straightens, jaw tense. I want to make sure I have his attention, let him know he has mine, but I hope my move isn't too bold.

Connelly likes to be the pursuer. He makes the move, not the other way around. He's the dominant man over the more dominant woman. I might've just angered him. Though, that anger could work to my advantage, too.

For the first time, his eyes meet mine. Dark pools of liquid black, they stare into me, a challenge. Keeping my facade in place, my guard up, I lick my lips deliberately. Watch his gaze fall lower to take in my subtle taunt. A hungry glint flashes in his eyes as he rests his hand, just a finger, over his mouth to hide a smile.

Coy. Charming. Oh, how the girls must eat up his act.

But this is good. I've pushed him just the right amount, letting him know I'm approachable, but I've left the ball in his court. He's still the one in charge, the shot caller. He's employing his tactics on me, which means I'm in his crosshairs.

He won't make a move on me in here, in front of others. The chance to be publically rejected is still too intimidating. He knows better from past experiences, and has learned to corner his prey, isolate them. He hates being humiliated. Even, or *especially*, by a filthy whore.

As his gaze continues to rake over me, now that I've invited his assessment, I can feel the chilly fingers of apprehension clutching at my boundaries. I should be more than wary. I should be afraid. If Quinn knew where I was right now, if he was aware of the dangerous game I'm playing, he would be furious. And disappointed. Maybe even a little insulted. Despite his stern act with me, he does hold me in high regard as a young woman of the law, and the fact that I'm debasing myself to get on the same level as a deviant offender says more than he'll ever know about the person I really am.

Some truths are better kept in the dark.

But I've tumbled in the filth with Connelly's likeness before. I discovered a long time ago just how deviant my nature can be. I no longer know where my boundaries are, where my hard limits lie. All I know for sure is that I will do what it takes to stop him from torturing one more girl.

Toying with a lock of my hair, I give him a smile of my own, encouraging him to finally make his move. He shifts in his seat, but doesn't stand. I follow his cues, waiting for him to stand so I can follow him out. Right when I think he's about to rise, his face hardens and my view is blocked. Someone steps in my line of vision.

"Seen you here a few times now."

I glance up into the face of a tall man with sun-weathered creases surrounding his glassy eyes. Timidly smiling, I say, "I've seen you, too."

"Well, then," he says, becoming bolder. He moves his pool stick aside and extends his hand. "We're overdue for an introduction. Why don't you join us for a game? We need another pretty face at the table."

I glance around him to see one of the girls bending

over the pool table to make a shot. Then I look at the guy's outstretched hand. "Sorry, honey. I don't play."

This needs to move along quickly. Connelly will be offended if I shrug off his subtle advance for another man. I could lose what little connection I've made with him.

The guy, who's wearing a plaid shirt and baseball hat, wraps his hand around my wrist and pulls me up to stand. "I don't mind teaching you a few things one bit, sweetheart."

Shit. Trying not to make a scene, I wrench my wrist free and smile. "Maybe I'll just watch. Root for you to win." I peek at Connelly. He's downing his SoCo, attention intentionally averted.

"That sounds real nice," the guy says. "Stick close to me, baby. I need a good luck charm." He winks as he settles his large hand at the small of my back.

My whole body locks up. Tension gathers in my shoulders, snaps my spinal cord straight. My skin flames where he his hot palm rests. As he guides me toward the pool table, I instinctually pull away from him, unable to suppress the flaring panic.

Pull it together, Sadie. The plaid-shirted trucker doesn't notice my aversion to being touched, but to my dread, Connelly does. There, in the pits of his black eyes, a twinkle of suspicion. A hint of doubt.

He's too fucking perceptive. A true hunter. This trucker might know a little about stalking, but he's light-years apart from the forensic tech who dissects and analyzes his prey down to their most basic, visceral need.

A sex worker who cringes at touch is either an intriguing specimen for him…or a red flag. As I settle in beside the trucker, I keep Connelly in my peripheral. I can almost see his brain churning the prospect; how excited he is by the thought of a woman, who's terrified of being touched, bound and tortured. Her fear that much more palpable. The inflicted pain felt that much more deeper.

Pure lust washes over his face, and he's having a difficult time controlling the tremor in his hand as he tips the tumbler to his mouth.

Caught.

After a week of fruitless foreplay, in one unguarded moment, I've become his ultimate target. By revealing my greatest vulnerability, I've ensnared a predator that rivals even my abductor.

This will end tonight.

"Scoot closer, baby." The trucker squeezes my waist, forcing my body close to his. "This game is about to get interesting."

My heart rate jacks, but I don't move. Frozen in place, I allow Connelly to assess me openly. My triggers and my reactions. My weaknesses. I'm giving him a wealth of knowledge to use against me, but it's a fair trade.

I'm learning even more about him.

Our desires can be our ultimate weakness, too.

The man at the other end of the pool table catches my

attention. He's sussing out his own target. He sways to the side on a drunken stagger as he raises his pool cue. As his partner leans over the table to line up her shot, he slides the stick between her legs.

She misses the shot, the tip of the cue marking the green felt. "Shit!" she snaps, glancing back at the guy. "That's fucking stupid. I'm on your team, ya know."

But he's not worried one bit about the game. He continues to run the stick up the inside of her thigh, then lifts the hem of her skirt, his gaze steady on his prize. When she attempts to straighten, he moves quickly. Bracing his hand against her back, he pushes her chest-down on the table.

My stomach clenches. Out of reflex, I place my hand on my hip, seeking the comfort of my weapon...only to find my SIG not there.

Her yelp startles the rest of the patrons of the bar, including Connelly. All eyes shift to watch the scene unfold as the drunk trucker yanks up her skirt. I wait, breath bated, for someone to stop this from happening.

Only no one does.

One by one, the patrons shake their heads, and either return to their drinking or stand to leave. As her warnings turn into shouts of protest, the bar clears out. Tightness squeezes my lungs, a vise-like terror infusing my chest.

This has happened before—and it's common.

A normal enough occurrence that a head shake or

distaste expressed through simply leaving and turning a blind eye is customary.

And why would anyone care what happens to a whore? Why waste the energy to stand up for her? She's looking for it. Asking for it. Sex is her profession.

This is why the Roanoke serial killer has gone unapprehended for almost three years. No one cares enough to investigate the murder of a sex worker, or even to report her missing. Who knows how many victims there actually are?

The country music pumping out of the old jukebox twangs on as the girl is stripped of her tank top. Ripped from her body, her faded pink bra is torn and hangs from one shoulder. Her breasts spring free to encourage the guy on.

Next to me, the plaid-shirted trucker hoots. "Get in there, Rusty! She's been begging for that dick."

A sickness coats my stomach as he pulls me in front of him, pinning me between the pool table and his erection. His sour beer breath caresses my cheek as he leans in close to my ear. "How about a freebie, honey. One for the road."

I have a badge in my car. I have a gun in my car. I have the power to stop this. One swift kick to his balls, and I can overpower him. At least for the seconds needed to gain the upper hand. Then run out of the bar. Get my badge and gun. Put in a call to have these rapists apprehended.

The local precinct might not warrant a rape of a sex

worker as a major sex crime, but attacking an agent? That would not be overlooked so easily.

My body is braced to put these thoughts into action—my hands gripping the edge of the pool table, my muscles strung tight, limbs ready to be put into motion—until I meet his eyes.

Black pools gauging me. Waiting to see my response.

I loathe myself because, as the girl screams, trying to fight off her attacker, I'm torn. Save one sex worker from being raped, allowing a serial killer to go free. Or witness the injustice and gain a chance to bring Lyle Connelly down.

In the moments it takes for me to weigh my options, the trucker behind me has my dress ruched up around my hips. He pushes his hand against my back, flattening my stomach against the scratchy green felt. Panic immobilizes my body, and it's enough time for him to spread my legs and step between them, removing my power.

As his fingers snake beneath my underwear, running the length of the seam across my ass to my core, a fierce quake erupts over my body. I watch the girl at the other end of the table submit. Tears leak from the corner of her eye, dripping into her destroyed hair, as her attacker pins her arms and thrusts into her.

Anger seizes me, spiking my blood. I take one last glimpse at Connelly. His eyes widen as I give away my intentions. Mine tell him everything he needs to know. *I will get you. This isn't over.* Then I reach for the pool cue in the center of the table, my fingers scraping and clawing the felt.

Just as my fingers nudge it, a hand snags it out of my grasp.

Connelly slits his eyes at me, a rye smile twists his lips —I'm made.

Then the pool stick makes contact with my attacker. A loud *crack*, then I'm released. Freed as the trucker shouts, "Fuck!"

I roll over and bring my feet in, then land both feet to his chest, kicking him backward as he holds his face. He stumbles into a table, and Connelly is there to finish him. He raises the broken pool cue over his head and proceeds to beat the trucker over the back of his head until he goes still.

The swift commotion garners the attention of the whole bar, which is now quiet and transfixed. I glance back at the girl. The guy has left her and is now coming after Connelly.

He lands a blow to Connelly's kidney, dropping him to the floor. On his knees, Connelly sweeps the blood-coated pool stick and takes out the trucker's legs. Once he's back on his feet, he sends a rapid kick to the trucker's stomach, then another to his head.

Shaky with adrenaline, I rush over to my attacker and feel for a pulse. He's alive. Knocked the hell out, but he'll live.

It hits me suddenly; Connelly is a hero. If this is called

in, he might be locked up for a night. Assault and battery charges placed. But once it's determined that he was defending a woman against rapists, the charges will be dropped to a misdemeanor. He might even walk with no charges. Connelly will be praised within his department for his heroics.

And I'll be sanctioned.

One word of this reaches Quinn and he'll know exactly what I've been up to. Working undercover with no authorization to do so. I didn't get clearance; I set out on this UC operation alone. I'm not sure if he'll be angrier that I ignored his order to stop investigating Connelly, or the fact that I put myself in danger.

Probably both.

A throaty whimper draws my attention. The waitress has the victimized girl wrapped in her thick arms, pulling her tattered shirt up over her shoulders. One look at them and I know this won't be reported. The girl doesn't want the law involved, and neither do the bar employees.

Here, the law is considered more of an enemy than the rapists who just attacked us.

I try to compose my facial features to resemble the downturned, resolute appearance of the two women. Though I know I'm not fooling Connelly, I have to keep my guise in place until I know for sure what happens next.

Connelly doesn't discard the pool cue. It's evidence, and he's a specialist that knows the evidence is damning. He takes it with him as he walks over to his table, removes his wallet, and drops a bill on the table. He doesn't look at anyone as he leaves the bar.

As the adrenaline ebbs, my rational mind comes back into play.

I'm not sure if this is a good thing or not; if I'm relieved or repulsed. I've studied Connelly for a month. Have worked the profile to understand his character, and his actions tonight deter from every conceivable outcome.

What's worse than not being able to predict the next move of a killer? Knowing that you and the killer are the only two enlightened by the truth.

I could rationalize that his dominant nature spurred him to act against his natural impulses. He claimed me as his, and refused to allow another man to tarnish his possession.

If he hadn't made me as an imposter, that very well could've been his motivation.

But there's something stronger at play here than his need: his survival instincts.

For those who revel in the taking of lives, they value and protect their own with a fierceness that rivals the protective nature of a mother over her child.

I let these thoughts fall into the background of my mind as I collect myself. Straightening my dress, I tug it down my thighs, smooth my disarrayed hair along my shoulders. The awkward silence filling the bar follows me as I move toward the table to grab my clutch and then head to the door. I won't be back to this bar, but neither will Connelly.

Before I leave the comforting light beaming from the lamppost, I remove my phone from my bag and poise my thumb over the lit screen, ready to hit my programed emergency button.

The rental car parked in the lot backs my story of my car being broken down, but also gives me another layer of anonymity. As I punch in the keyless entry code under the door handle, an eerie feeling touches the back of my neck.

I open the door and have one foot inside the car when I feel a rough band of rope circle my neck. Shock grips me and I gasp—but I was ready; I hold on to that single, nearly fleeting thought as I prepare to lose my ability to breathe. I'm primed for him to deflect my attempt to grab the rope, so I focus on my phone, my thumb already moving over the screen.

"I've been studying you, too." His words are a low rasp as he wraps his hand around my wrist. Before I can hit the button, he rams my arm against the car. My phone drops to the gravel.

I squeeze my eyes closed, dragging in a breath past the constriction of my throat.

He closes the door, then pulls my back against his chest as he drags me away from the car. The sudden loss of the interior light submerges us in the cover of darkness. The chirr of crickets seems to grow louder, hostile, as if the insects are provoked by the intruders invading their woods.

My heel snags on a root. The shoe is lost to the soggy ground. I concentrate on keeping the other one in place; a possible weapon.

Once we're out of eyeshot, the tall grass and trees obscuring us from the bar, I'm forced to my knees. The muddy earth is cold and biting against my skin. He loosens the rope enough for me to take an unobstructed breath. I suck in the taste of dirt and humid summer as I fill my lungs.

The press of a sharp object at my waist causes me to flinch out of reflex.

"That's not really your style," I say, trying to buy time —to get him talking. To do anything but use that knife.

The blade is removed, but the rope tightens around my neck. Blood rushes my ears in a *whoosh* as pressure bulges my eyes. My fingers dig at the coarse rope, trying to find access beneath the tightly bound cord. Then just as I fear losing consciousness, he loosens his grip.

The rope slides against my neck as I gasp in air around a cough, the feel of choking still clinging to my throat.

I watch his booted feet appear in my vision, the moonlight glinting off the polished, rubbed black. I keep my eyes on the ground as he stops before me.

"There are witnesses," I say.

"None of which give a damn about either of us."

"You know my death will be investigated. I'm not one

of your victims; I won't simply disappear." I look up into his face then. Stare into the shadowed sockets of his dark eyes.

"There won't be a body to investigate." Connelly runs the pad of his thumb over the tip of the blade.

I open my mouth to say more, to let him know who I am, how Detective Quinn and the task force will link my disappearance to him—but the knife makes contact with the collar of my dress, pressing into my skin and stifling my words.

As Connelly kneels in the mud, his weapon gouging into my flesh, I force my eyes not to close. I hold his gaze as he slices a clean cut down the fabric. The sound of tearing material sends me right back into my nightmarish memories.

Sweat trickles into the shallow cut on my chest with a biting sting…then he rips the collar away, revealing my neck and chest. With another swift move, he slips the flat of the blade beneath my bra. The cold steel assaults my skin. I shiver, and that entices a smile from his twisted lips. He turns the knife and yanks, cutting my bra away from my body.

His eyes assess the my scar. And as he says, "Oh, beauty. How divine your torture must've been," I hold the gaze of the killer before me. I will not look away. I will not give him the fear he feasts on.

His fingers test the scar tissue along my collarbone. Lust flickers in his eyes as his hand trails up to capture the necklace around my neck. "I rarely take such an obvious trophy," he says, wrapping the chain around his hand. "But I can't resist."

He jerks the necklace from my neck and then pushes me to the ground.

The chirr of the crickets crescendos as I stare up at the star-painted sky through the canopy of treetops. So heavenly. So transcendent. So far removed from this moment.

SADIE

Red.

The color of the breaking morning sky through my windshield.

Fire red. Angry red. Love red… It can be perceived so many ways, with so many conflicting emotions.

The sun's fiery rays kiss the clouds, emblazoning the stretch of cool black with a sweet caress of warmth red.

Or

The rising sun slashes the sky with violent streaks, consuming the peaceful night with blistering fire red.

It's deceptive, this bold color. Amorous and full of fervor, it paints the still dawn in shades that denote tranquility.

But the fire surging up within me is anything but tranquil.

It rages. Like a bolt of lightning striking on the horizon, my vision is rimmed with a pulsing red as the sky deepens in intensity. Her face is there—etched in pain and horror—against my eyelids every time I blink away the rising sun.

Avery.

The tires rumble against the asphalt as I push down on the pedal, gaining speed over the highway. The sound of flipping pages makes my jaw clench, and I grip the steering wheel tighter. To my right, Colton is searching each member file of The Lair.

It's unlikely that the UNSUB is in those files. It's possible that he found access into the top levels of the club another way. Paying off a bouncer. Stealing an identity. Simply sneaking past all detection.

But I have to trust Quinn's method here: follow each lead until we reach the end. We have to analyze every member—only I'm so terrified we're already out of time.

Avery.

Applying more pressure to the accelerator, I weave my Honda in and out of traffic, zipping past honking cars as they pull off to the side.

Somehow, I made her a target. Her proximity to me at work couldn't be the only reason the UNSUB chose to abduct her. There's more, another purpose. There has to be.

Her last message to me feels as if it's burning a hole in my jacket pocket. The need to pull the note out and read it again consumes me. I've already studied it, trying to discern some meaning, some code...

Colton's touch draws me out of my frenzied thoughts, and I expel a shaky breath.

"You'll find her," he says, his hand giving my thigh a comforting squeeze. "Ease off the gas, Sadie. You can't help anyone if we wreck."

Nodding, I lick my lips and slowly lift my foot. "Did you find anything...anyone?"

"Two potentials so far." Colton releases me and resumes his search. "I'm starting with location first. Anyone who has lived in the downstate area over the past three years, and who's recently moved here. Although you said the UNSUB would be aware of law enforcement methods. So if he's in here, I doubt he gave us truthful information."

Right. Exactly. The profile states a lot of things that are in direct conflict with our current course of action. We have to go against logic here, because the UNSUB is aware of the profile, too. He's known every move within the department before we've made it. And he's predicting our next.

"By abducting Avery, he's counting on me making a mistake," I say. "I'm too close. He knows I've made a connection, and he's trying to rattle me. Trying to force me into making a mistake."

"Then don't." Colton closes a file and turns toward me.

His gaze penetrates my defenses, and just for a moment, I feel the burn of tears behind my eyes. In this car's intimate confines, I don't have to pretend. I don't have to be brave or distant, shutting out an unsure, threatening world.

I've kept myself locked in that basement, afraid. Alone. Unwilling to trust. If I ever lowered my walls, I'd only find myself right back there. But it was always a threat against *me*—*my* fear. I never once thought someone else would take my place.

I would switch with Avery in a heartbeat if I could.

"Oh, my god." Flipping the blinker, I pull off the highway and onto the long stretch of road that wraps the ACPD building.

"What is it?" Colton is already collecting the files and the amended profile I hastily compiled back at The Lair.

I park in the closest space to the front doors, ignoring the posted, assigned name. I go through the motions of putting the car in Park and killing the engine, stuffing evidence into my bag, my mind on autopilot.

"Sadie?"

I find and hold Colton's gaze, frightened of this realization. "He wants me, Colton."

His expression shutters as his striking features pull into hard lines. "He's not going to—"

"No," I say, shaking my head. "He wants *me*. Not Avery. The *why* or the *for what* isn't important. Not anymore. I can't waste time trying to uncover his delusion. But I can use it. I can make him believe he'll get what he wants."

"What the hell are you saying? That you'll use yourself as bait? Fuck that... No."

"It wouldn't be the first time...and I'm trained. I have field experience and I'm the most qualified to deal with the UNSUB on a psychological platform. And—" I reach over and take his hand "—it has to be part of the reason why he chose Avery. He wants me to take her place."

"That's exactly why you are not doing it." His voice is raw, grating against my resolve.

"I don't have time to look for another answer. This is the only way to get her back alive."

Our eyes stay locked, time seemingly suspended around us by this defining moment. I'm not asking his permission; my mind is already made up. I'm simply letting him know my choice. Hoping he will support me, regardless of what it will cost us.

"You're not the only one he wants, goddess." His hand cups my cheek, his palm rough, yet strong and comforting against my skin.

I shut my eyes. Feel his strength and determination. "I know. But he wants you out of the way. It's not the same. His revenge for me goes deeper." As I open my eyes, I'm decided. "I can save Avery."

"And you will," he says. "But I refuse to lose you—in

any way, shape or form. Whether it's physically or mentally...I won't lose one single piece of you to him."

He dips toward my knees and pushes the lever beneath my seat. As I'm propelled backward away from the steering wheel, his sure hands clasp my waist. In one swift, strong move, he has me over the console and on his lap.

"Colton..." I lower my chin, letting my hair conceal my face. "There's no time—"

He palms my face, forcing my eyes to meet his intense blue gaze. "There's always time for us. Especially when it comes to making you understand that I will never let you sacrifice yourself." His lips crash against mine, stealing my breath and replacing my heartache with need.

My arms circle his neck as I pull him close, unable to sate the sudden, unbearable yearning to connect with him. Be a part of him. For him to chase away the fear, the fury, and protect me from the past reaching up from the corners of my mind to haunt me.

But I can't be lost. No matter how badly I crave oblivion, Colton makes me *feel*. From the moment he first touched me, first branded me, I couldn't ignore those overpowering emotions, despite how foreign they were. I am no longer teetering on the edge of two worlds—I am wholly and irrevocably his. I'm home.

I belong.

As he deepens the kiss, he grasps my nape, bringing me closer still. His hard want presses against me, ratcheting my desire. He moves to my neck, and I suck in a breath past the onslaught of sensations as his free hand travels under my dress, up my thigh, possessively caressing the ache between my legs.

He breaks away to whisper against my lips, "I need to hear you say it. Tell me you won't do anything to put yourself in danger." His heated gaze sears me. "Promise me, Sadie."

I bite my lip, desperate to give myself over to him—to assuage the fear I feel drumming beneath my hand as his heart beats wildly. But it's not a promise I can make. I don't know where this will lead or end.

He expels a heavy breath, rests his forehead against mine. "This isn't a request, goddess—it's a demand. I need to know we'll make it through this—"

"We will," I say, gripping his shirt, my hand fisted so tightly around the material my knuckles ache.

His mouth seals over mine, coaxing the promise from me in his own way. I can feel his intent with each lip-crushing kiss. His tongue whispers his vow as he strokes the seam of my mouth, then dives deeper until our breath becomes one desperate plea between us.

"Come for me," he says. "I need to make you come."

A jolt of awareness rushes me. I glance around the parking lot. It's early…vacant, but— Colton arrests my senses before I can object, expertly working my underwear aside.

"Don't tell me no," he says as the rough pads of his fingers slip into my sensitive folds. He finds my center and

31

pushes inside, releasing a groan at the feel of my slick arousal for him. "This is what you need—what I need. I'll never deny you. It's not selfish, goddess. Not when we're designed differently."

I grip his hair, undulating my hips on top of him as he shamelessly brings me to the edge. His thumb swirls over my clit as I grind against him, the feel of his erection, his desire for me, making me bold.

I attempt to check the parking lot, but he seizes my gaze, his grip in my hair forcefully commanding my face toward his. "Look at me. Not them. Don't be afraid of who you really are, goddess. We play by different rules. Always above them, because we embrace our dark deeds. Never denying ourselves. Not anymore."

His mouth captures the band of rope around my wrist, his teeth tightening the cord until it bites into my skin. The coarse fibers graze my flesh, heightening every sensation. My eyes close as I slip into ecstasy.

A soft moan escapes my lips as I break and he's there to catch it, his mouth swallowing my release as he drinks me in.

As I come down, the climax fading into ripples of pleasure skittering over my skin, I open my eyes. "I'm terrified," I admit.

The knot of his throat bobs on a hard swallow. "You're not leaving me. I promise you that."

"And I'm not losing you," I say, letting the desperation leak from my voice.

His eyes narrow. "Never."

"Then you have to trust me to do what I have to in order to help Avery."

Another heavy breath, then, "We'll talk about this later, when Quinn can back me up on how crazy this is and that it's not ever happening. I can at least count on him for that." His firm expression morphs into confusion. "Wait. What did you say before? That it wouldn't have been the first time... What aren't you telling me?"

My lips part, my mouth dry—the words right on the tip of my tongue. Colton has bared his soul to me, has trusted me with his darkest secret. A secret that would destroy his life if it were ever revealed. It's the kind of secret that would shatter any other two people—but not us.

It binds us together. Makes us the same—if only just.

But that's the distinction. The very narrow disparity that casts him in light, and keeps me shrouded by darkness. The crucial variable that separates us.

What he did in his past was out of love, compassion, and mercy. My choices...my actions...were purely executed out of revenge. Loathing. Despair. Colton deserves to know the truth of me, but god, I'm terrified. So fucking terrified to stand before him with complete transparency.

"Goddess..." His fingers rove over my face, his eyes seeking a crack in my armor.

"Not here," I finally say. Taking a deep breath, I revel in his touch a moment longer. I know he'll wait for me—

but there is an expiration date. And it's approaching fast. "I need to be focused on Avery right now. But I promise…"

"I'm patient, Sadie. As long as it takes." Then his lips are on mine, slowly and tenderly caressing my fears away. I cling to him, to that promise. I cling so hard I can taste the loss in his kiss. What I will lose when the time comes. A deep pang hollows out my chest as the truth of it crushes me.

I can't lose this. I only just found him.

A swell of blaring sirens breaks us apart, and I whip around to see squad cars rushing past. "We have to go. Quinn's gathering the task force."

The mood inside the department is fragile. Tension suffocates the air, strangling the camaraderie. Where a strike against one of our own should band us together, creating a unified, unstoppable force, there's a looming current of suspicion that threatens to unravel the department.

The UNSUB could be one of us.

It seethes in the looks I get as I hurry through the bullpen. It festers in the chaos crippling an otherwise structured task force. I understand why I'm being targeted; I've been barred from the case, and now I'm pushing my way through with a suspect at my side. Not only did I get Colton released from questioning, but I'm including him— an outsider—in the investigation.

When all this is over, I'll be reprimanded. Maybe even discharged and investigated myself. There's a chance—a very likely chance—that I'll be found guilty of obstruction…or worse. But none of that matters just as long as I can bring Avery back.

As I turn the corner toward my office, I spot Quinn. His eyes widen a second before he's gunning for me. It feels like this morning has lasted a week already. As if it's been much longer than the hour it's taken to get Quinn up to speed on Avery's situation and for Colton and me to reach the station.

Quinn hands off a document to a uniform and steps in my path. "My office. Now." His attention is momentarily diverted toward Colton. "You—" He points toward a chair. "Sit and go nowhere."

"We don't have time for this shit, Quinn," I say, trying and failing to get around his sizable form. "We can do this however you want…but later. Avery is all that matters right now."

I look up into his rugged face, my eyes pleading. I don't have the strength to be angry, or demanding. I will beg on Avery's behalf. Quinn's gaze softens, and I can see the misery and worry he's suffered since the news of Avery's abduction hit.

"My office, Bonds."

I glance back at Colton and nod firmly. "Please continue to—"

"I'm on it." He holds up the files.

I offer him a grateful smile before I'm escorted into Quinn's office. I turn, my mouth already parted as I prepare to defend my place on the task force, but the sight of Lyle Connelly steals my breath. A blown-up image of his face hangs on Quinn's whiteboard. A collection of data about his whereabouts is scattered around his photo. Red string connects points on a map, denoting sightings.

"So you did hear me," I say, walking toward the clear board. "I knew you would look into him. You put this together last night?"

"I started it…but I didn't dig in until Avery. Jesus, Sadie. Tell me what the fuck is going on." I turn to see him drive a hand through his hair, his blue tie hanging loose over a rumpled white shirt.

An ache blisters the back of my throat. "I need to tell you—"

"No, you know what?" He storms toward me and anchors his large hands to my arms, holding me securely before him. "Don't tell me. Don't say a word."

"Quinn, I have to—"

"Bonds, the only thing that counts right now, this second, is finding our M.E. You hear me? Do you understand?" His eyes fill with an alarming desperation, and his hands latch on harder, as if any word that passes my lips will tear me from his grasp. "I can't do anything with that information right now. Nothing. Because I need you on this case."

With a heavy sigh, he releases me and heads to his desk where he pulls out an evidence bag. He removes my phones and tosses me one and then the other.

Awkwardly, I catch both and grip them by my sides. "I'm back in? That simple?"

He nods once. "When we nail this bastard and Avery's safe, you know I'll have to investigate."

"I know." And I do. It has nothing to do with us—it's not personal. Quinn also swore an oath, but unlike me, he doesn't believe in gray areas. It's all black and white. He's always been by the book. I don't fault him at all.

"Until then…" He walks around the desk, his shoulders squared, his head higher despite his obvious exertion. "You're my partner on this."

I swallow the emotion clogging my throat. A stupid smile twists my lips despite my whole body and soul feeling as if I've been flayed. "Your partner? I thought you didn't do partners, Quinn. Especially profilers."

He shrugs a heavy shoulder. "You have what I need, Bonds." His gaze stays locked on mine as the weight of his statement hangs between us. "And I know that you'll do everything within your power to help Avery. That's good enough for me."

The air between us feels as fragile as the atmosphere outside this room. We're linked together by our shared desire to see Avery safe, and to capture the monster responsible for that threat. But it's a tenuous thread joining us—a single pull in either direction could snap it, and we both know that.

I glance through the glass wall at Colton scouring the files. I could've gone my whole life never truly knowing what it meant to be loved, needed. Adored. Trusted, and to be able to return that trust. I was always alone. Alone is safe.

I think about Avery…her face twisted in pain, all by herself.

Alone is not safe.

Alone is the most frightening place.

Avery will not stay alone.

I look into Quinn's eyes. "When this is over, I won't run."

"I know."

"But I won't make it easy."

"I know that, too."

I suck in a breath. "For the first time, I have something to lose. I'm going to fight for it."

He glances at Colton, a hard line creasing his mouth. "Are you sure he's worth it?"

"Absolutely."

With a forced exhale, Quinn nods resolutely. "All right. I just need to know…" He trails off, searching for the right phrasing. "Connelly's not good for this, is he? There's no way?"

I don't blink. "No. I'm positive. He's not the UNSUB."

As Quinn absorbs that truth, I can see the battle raging behind his walls. By trusting me, he's going against everything he stands for. "So then we're looking for someone connected to Connelly and the Roanoke killings."

I release a tense breath. "The profile on the Roanoke serial killer and Connelly's whereabouts during those three years puts Connelly at the scenes of all the cold cases. But he wasn't alone. He had a partner. It's as we speculated before; a master and servant. Connelly had an apprentice."

"So which is which?" he asks.

I hold his unyielding gaze. "The apprentice is our UNSUB."

TICK TOCK

UNSUB

Do you know who I am?

Let me tell you a story. The details will help you connect the pieces, and as my voice lulls you into a safe, warm haven, the clues will start to paint a picture.

I love our story. She'll enjoy it, too. Precious alabaster skin. Soft hair. Clear, crystal tears. Avery loves to hear me talk, because she's learned it's the only time I don't desire to hear her screams.

I confess; I don't usually take a liking to my pets. They're dispensable. A necessity, yes, but an entertainment that quickly loses amusement and continuously needs to be upgraded to achieve fulfillment. It's exhausting, really. The constant demand to find the next new, shinier toy.

41

I don't regard any of them enough to use their names. But this pet—Avery—is different. She's exquisite. She's important to my love, so therefore, important to me, and must be handled delicately. Reverently.

And as such, I run my fingers through her silky hair as I begin my tale. The story of *us*.

There's a bar tucked away on the outskirts of a city. It's completely unimportant. Could be any bar. Could be any city. But on this particular hunting night, with a sliver of moon nicking the black sky, it's the perfect setting.

I sat on a barstool and watched. As always. Bored and hoping he would choose quickly, I sipped at my drink as my agitation grew. The monotony was getting to me, see. After three years of grooming, I was confident I was ready to take charge. It would be nearly two years before I realized that he needed me more than I needed him, and this was his way of keeping me compliant. But regardless, I was yearning for something…*new*.

I'm not delusional enough to believe that this was the reason she walked through those doors, but she did all the same. Wearing a little red dress, just like the innocent child of the fated fairytale, she strode through the room, tempting all the big, bad wolves.

But she was no innocent.

She wore her color of power, of temptation, for one purpose: she was a hunter.

Like the deceptively poisonous Monarch that

purposely invites attention with its brilliancy, her beauty signaled a warning to predators. *Look but don't touch.*

Is she really dangerous, or is it a guise? Does her skin truly taste of venom, or is she as sweet as she looks…

My mouth watered. The question of her was enough to trigger every fascination.

There was only one truth to be sure of: she would complete me.

I wasn't the only enraptured beast that night in that dank little bar, hungering for her liquid green eyes to lay claim to me. But I was the only one to escape her shrewd, predatory gaze.

That's why I was chosen in the first place, after all. The wallflower. The unnoticed. The overlooked. My mentor convinced me this was a strength, not a weakness. He took me under his wing and transformed me. He molded me into a stealthy demon that crept in the shadows and sprang only when all elements aligned.

So on this night, while the huntress was stalking her prey, I was safely studying her from the sidelines. I didn't know then that it was in my power to stop what was to come. How could I?

You see, I was preoccupied. The murder of a city girl had shown a spotlight right on us. It had only been two months since my first kill—since my mentor granted me permission to demonstrate what I'd learned—and the details of the recent murder resembled my technique so closely that even my mentor was suspicious.

Was I out of control? Did I have no stamina? Was I going to get us caught?

I had to eliminate the technique stealing copycat to gain my master's favor again—to prove that I didn't violate our partnership. This hack imitator—whoever he was—would pay.

I was so sure of my talents. And ultimately, that was my undoing.

The vixen in the red dress didn't need to put me in her sights to destroy me. She was not like the Monarch, waiting to be devoured, patiently accepting her place in nature to wreak retribution. She was like the widow spider, the pursuer. Her fangs sank into my vein, and the poison spread to every connecting blood vessel, detonating a cataclysmic event that would shake the whole of me.

She was destruction incarnate.

I envied her. That wasn't an emotion I was comfortable with. Her performance surpassed mine...even my mentor's...and I wanted to snuff out the threat of something greater than us.

Connelly agreed, of course, but his reasoning was more logical. She was a different kind of threat to him, because she knew who he was, *what* he was. He was going to make an example of her, but first, he needed to disgrace her. Discredit her.

It was just all so entertaining, watching them toy with each other. I admit, I got a thrill out of it. Up until that point, no one had held a candle to my mentor. I was fixated, like a scientist on the brink of a discovery. I needed to observe.

Then, she walked right past me. The scent of lavender enveloped me, and I inhaled deeply. That's when I saw it. The crest. It hung from a chain around her neck. I glimpsed just a peek before she quickly tucked it beneath the blouse of her dress as she shook her dark hair from her shoulders.

Everything about her was carefully devised, deliberately meant to keep your focus on the obvious—the sex. She wielded it like a weapon. Guarded herself with beauty like a shield. All so perfectly designed to pull you into her trap…right before she escapes, leaving nothing of her true self behind. No lingering effect of her real person to call into question.

She was a delicious apparition who would haunt me forever if I didn't discover who she was. That one piece around her neck could open a world of knowledge for me about my temptress. It was the key to her.

But I digress. The point of this story, the moral, is that we can plan for a life, make endless preparations, have everything falling into place…and then *boom*! We're rocked. Our very foundation tested.

What we choose to do after the fact defines us.

My little red widow shook my world that night. That upset nearly catapulted me to ground zero. But I would rebuild. I would come back stronger, smarter, deadlier.

Instead of submitting to her venom, allowing it to

consume me whole—I festered in it, little by little, until I built up a tolerance. And once I was sure I could suffer her bite without succumbing to my weakness, I struck.

But on that night—the night that tipped the first domino—I watched. As always.

In the end, I made my mentor proud. I obeyed his command and suffered her poisonous attack in writhing agony.

Oh, how I would revel in my vengeance. How I would draw blood. How I would bleed her until her entire world ran red...

But first, I would unlock her secrets.

Avery stirs in my lap. I glance down, having almost forgotten the point of my story. My fingers dig into her hair and I yank her head up. Her whimper soothes the burn of that memory.

"I bet you don't know what I know," I whisper to her.

Her thick sobs send a shiver over my skin, and I wrap my other hand around her throat. Squeeze until her body is wracked with tremors.

Then with disgust, I shove her off and stand. She curls into a ball at my feet, her pathetic crying and the jangle of her chains suddenly grating my nerves.

"What is taking our Sadie so long?" I ask, not really seeking an answer.

I've patiently and painstakingly orchestrated the perfect scene...and my beauty is not keeping to the plan. It was the wrong move allowing them to take her communication away. It forced my hand, and I *hate* that. It was too soon.

With a deep inhale, I find my center. No one could've created what I have. No one could present Sadie with the perfect gift as I have done. So, no one can take this away from me.

With a grunt, I reach for the lever and crank the rig. The chains clang and rattle as they pull taut, dangling a thrashing Avery in the middle of my dungeon. Her pink tank top clings to her slick skin, her bare thighs glisten from hours of struggle. Her recently dyed brown hair layers her face, concealing just enough, tempting me to believe she *is* my love.

My cock hardens at the prospect, but no—not yet. She's an illusion. I want—I *will* have—the real thing.

I turn to leave so that Avery can experience what transformed my Sadie into the ultimate beauty, but a rumbling snags my attention. The phone on the table vibrates to life.

My excitement almost makes me trip over my own feet to get to it. And then...on the screen...in beautiful bold font, there she is.

Sadie: *You have something of mine, and I want it back.*

A wild laugh escapes me.

Me: *I've missed you.*

Sadie: *Then let's make a trade.*

My hands quake with my anticipation as I clutch the phone.

One more game, then checkmate.

APART

COLTON

"The signal is pinging all over the state," the tech behind the computer says. "He's using a proxy chain. No way to get an accurate trace."

Sadie curses as she stares down at her cell phone. "And he's not taking the bait. Dammit. I need to send a message that really tempts him."

Quinn holds up his hand. "He knows what we're trying to do."

"We have to try," she says. "I can convince him to meet with me. I just need more time…to be able to get inside his head."

She looks over at me, her eyes fierce. I know what's going through her mind. Her words say one thing to Quinn and the task force, and another entirely to me. When she makes her move away from them, I'll be there. I won't let her do this alone.

"He has to feel like he's the one in control," she continues, her thumbs flying over the on-screen keyboard. "As long as I stay in communication with him, keep his focus on me, he's not…" She trails off, pain flashing across her face. She clears her throat. "Then he's not focused on Avery."

"Letting the UNSUB be the shot caller is not what we want," Quinn says.

Sadie's gaze swings up. "He's a pathological narcissist who needs all attention to be on him. If it's not, if anything threatens his sense of control, he'll devolve. He'll become unpredictable, and I'm not letting that happen." Her glare narrows on Quinn. "Besides, he has Avery. He's absolutely the shot caller."

I glance between them, caught in the middle of their stare down, observing a battle of wills that must've started long before now. I'm tempted to back up Sadie—she knows more about this UNSUB's character than anyone here—but I know my place. And it's not in the line of fire. For now.

With a disgruntled sigh, Quinn caves. "Are we ready to give the updated profile to the task force?"

She finishes her text as the techs monitor each keystroke. "Yes." She looks up. "We're ready. I've already given the unis a short comparison sheet. I put them on the task of bringing in any suspect that matches that description. I want every possible offender put in holding while I'm able to keep in contact with the UNSUB."

"We don't have the resources or the time to hunt down every suspect and bring them in, Bonds," Quinn roars.

Sadie moves to stand at the front of the conference room, a whirl of chaos rushing around her. She's the calm center of a storm in the midst of crashing waves; they break against her, but she's the rock holding strong against the tide. She's beautiful.

"Make it happen," she snaps. "We're wasting time arguing over it. I need to get out of here and—"

"And go where?" Quinn steps closer to her, and my hands curl into fists at my sides. "This entire building has already been processed. I've told you this."

She stares right back at him. "Not by me it hasn't."

Quinn shakes his head. "What are you hoping to find that CSU hasn't?"

"I don't know, Quinn—I'll know it when I see it. And right now, we have nothing else." Her bottom lip trembles, just for a second. Just a peek into the doubt and heartache clashing inside her.

That one glimpse at her pain sends me to her side, earning me a cool glare from Quinn. "She's right. You know she needs to be the one to head this up."

Sticking my neck out in front of Quinn isn't the smartest move. Especially when there's a piece of evidence in the form of a letter from the UNSUB addressed to me in my pocket. But there's an understanding between Quinn and me. He's not calling into question her knowledge on the case or her ability to work it; he's concerned for her safety. That concern, however, is going to cost Avery her life if he doesn't trust himself to protect Sadie.

I uncovered that insecurity during our tense ride to the station when he threatened me to stay away from her. It was a revealing moment between us that put a bad taste in my mouth.

But he doesn't respond to me. Glowering past me, he addresses Sadie. "If he's going to remain here, he goes into a box. He's not helping otherwise. And technically, he's still a suspect." Quinn crosses his arms, making his point.

"I'm not going back into interrogation," I say, matching his stance.

"Christ," Sadie says. She hands the phone to the main tech, then turns toward us. "He's not responding anymore." Placing her hands to her forehead, she pushes her hair back, her agitation apparent. To Quinn, she says, "You said we were partners on this. And as such, that requires trust."

His features harden into an impenetrable expression as he holds Sadie's stare. It's as if something of a deeper meaning passes between them, and I try hard to keep my resentment in check.

"Do you trust me?"

Quinn releases his stubborn will with a long exhale. His shoulders deflate. "Yes. I trust you."

"Then don't question my leads. Please." The pleading in her voice is enough to break any man. "We have to work together on this. It's the only way. I'll work the potential abduction sites, while you compare the members of the club that Colton flagged against—" she lowers her voice "—against the department. Use the profile as the control."

Quinn's eyes widen. "There's no way to do that incognito. I need us *all* working as a team, and dissidence will put a halt to that real quick." He stuffs his hands in his pockets. "No better way to throw a wrench in the system than to start pointing fingers."

Sadie nods. "Let me handle that part. Just try to find a way to run searches without alerting Wexler or anyone else."

Again, Quinn stares at Sadie for a long moment before he agrees. "All right." Then he turns toward the room and takes in the anarchy that has descended over the task force. "Get in line, people! We have new information."

I move to the back of the room and lean against the wall as the officers find seats. Every ear is piqued as Quinn prepares to address his task force.

"This case is no longer about catching a serial killer. It's about bringing home one of our own." He nods to a cop at the front of the room, and he proceeds to place three enlarged portraits of the bound and gagged woman from my phone on the giant whiteboard.

The air is alive with tension as the sudden, stark silence charges the room.

"Avery Johnson is a top medical examiner in her field. She's worked with the ACPD for more than five years, and what's more, she's family." A rumble of acknowledgement flows through the room. "We're bringing her home."

Quinn adjusts his stance, getting into his leader mode. I have to admit, he's good at it. "Avery disappeared sometime between the night before last and early this morning. She's presumed to have been missing for at least ten hours. We know the next twenty-four hours of this case is crucial. Therefore, we do not sleep, eat, drink, piss, or shit until we have a break in this case. And we're going to follow Agent Bonds' profile to the letter." He glances over at her and nods.

My heart jumps into my throat as Sadie takes the floor. She's tiny compared to Quinn, but every inch of her radiates authority. She's wearing the dress she had on last night, with my leather jacket zipped up to conceal most of it.

"The UNSUB we're hunting was once part of a partnership," she begins. "A killing team. He built his original identity on the foundation of that bond, and therefore feels out of sorts working alone. It's the reason he devolved so rapidly once he started the killing cycle again. He's seeking a connection with another individual in which he can rebuild that team dynamic."

Her gaze settles on me for a brief second, her eyes

harboring the truth of her words. The UNSUB has already found someone to try to form that relationship with. Sadie. This has all been to gain her attention, and in a warped manner, her approval. In some morbid way, this guy looks at it like foreplay. My back teeth grind.

"He was dependent on his mentor, and the loss of that relationship caused an upset which manifested in identity confusion," she continues. "His methodology evolved as he tried to discover his own style without a teacher. We see that result in his copycat approach to an ideal serial killer."

A hand goes up, and Sadie nods to the officer. "Why did the UNSUB select the Blood Countess, Agent Bonds? There're so many other serial killers to choose from. Do we have insight into a connection there?"

My discomfort reflects Quinn's tense form.

Sadie lifts her head a notch higher. "That's a question of the chicken and the egg." At the confused grumble echoing around the room, she clarifies. "Did the UNSUB first select Bathory to emulate, then seek out a connection? Or did he search within our department first to establish a correlation?" She takes a breath. "Truthfully, I'm not sure. The only thing I know positively is that he is a narcissist who must control his environment. My knowledge and expertise on the Bathory murders gave him the foothold he needed to build upon. Once that connection within the department was made, he used it as his narcissistic supply. What better way to garner attention than to tap directly into the source?

"Pathological narcissists have a grandiose sense of self. Their need for admiration outweighs their every other need, and their lack of empathy means others will suffer because of it. Our UNSUB is a malignant narcissist who seeks omnipotence, and will attempt to achieve this by any means. He must be in control. Therefore, our authority is a direct threat to him."

Notes are jotted down while this information resonates.

"The UNSUB is comfortable in victims' homes, as well as outside in the open. He's a psychopathic sexual sadist who uses a victim's home—her place of shelter and safety—against her to dominate her in her own element and increase her fear.

"This particular deviant offender is organized and methodical, but because he needs to be seen in a god-like manner, he suffers to maintain his own delusion. He's structured his world by a set of rituals that he must fulfill to keep his delusion sound. His fiction involving the Countess Bathory ties him to this department, and the abduction of Avery—an insider to us—stresses his desire to overthrow what he views as the ultimate authority and make it his own."

Another hand goes up. "Where do we start looking?"

Sadie rolls her shoulders. "Offenders who suffer from this specific narcissism are prone to work in economics, politics, and even medicine. Pathological or malignant narcissists are also drawn to careers in law. Such as lawyers...or law enforcement itself." Tension thrums heavily among the body of officers. "Because of his inside knowledge on the workings of this department, it's not an assumption that he has direct access. Either to someone here, or as a member himself."

Of all people, Detective Carson speaks up. "But couldn't he be obtaining his information from the leak? I mean, just about the whole world has insider knowledge now thanks to that."

Carson. That smug asshole feels he's above raising his hand. If anyone in this department fits the profile, it's that douchebag.

Sadie seems to agree as she cuts her eyes at him, but she quickly checks herself. "If he's not working directly with the ACPD, then yes, he could likely be in contact with the leak."

Carson jumps in again. "Then if we find the leak, we can locate the UNSUB, right? Why aren't we profiling the leak, Agent Bonds? Seems just as logical."

"Our effort is best spent on discovering the identity of the UNSUB, Detective Carson. We need all focus on him and bringing Avery back alive." She presses on before Carson can interrupt. "Which leads us to the next leg of this investigation. Deducing what we know from his previous partner."

"Wait," Carson says, standing. "We have this information? Since when?"

"Since now." Quinn moves to the forefront. "There's already a team working the angle of this suspect. Due to the leak in the department—" he eyes Carson "—this task force is on a need-to-know basis as new information develops."

Quinn clears is throat. "The UNSUB is suspected of being involved with the serial killings that went cold two years ago in Roanoke. I have a packet for each member of the task force that elaborates on this profile and the evidence we need to uncover to determine the UNSUB's identity."

"Is the UNSUB still in contact with Agent Bonds?" another officer asks.

Quinn goes to answer, but Sadie intercepts the question. "Yes. We're going to continue to use this tactic to keep communication open about Avery's condition."

"That's it, people," Quinn says. "Most of you already have your instructions. The rest proceed to the front to get your assignments. We're going to get this sadistic perp, and we're going to save Avery. Get to work!"

The room breaks apart in a chaotic but orderly fashion, every person hustling to get back on the case. I move toward the front of the room. I'm not on the task force. I'm the furthest thing from a cop there is…but I'll do whatever I can to help Sadie. I know Quinn and the others have her back, will do everything in their power to keep her safe during this—but they're also working within the law to do so.

If it comes down to it, they have to make their choices

according to regulations, and that could complicate their duty. My only duty is to Sadie.

She will take every risk to save her friend, and I will take every risk to make sure she walks away alive. Quinn and Carson can measure their pricks along the black and white sideline for all I care. I won't hesitate when it comes to her.

"What the hell is he doing here?" Carson says as I approach. "We've got a fucking leak, but we're just letting suspect civilians have inside access?"

Quinn directs his attention on me. "He's providing information on The Lair." He looks at Carson. "And he's your new informant. He's riding with you to bring in suspects."

"What?" I say.

"The hell?" Carson follows up.

My chest ignites. The thought of separating from Sadie signals a huge red flag. "I'm not leaving Sadie."

"I don't like it. But maybe it isn't such a bad idea," Carson says with a slight smirk. "Keep him in custody where I can keep an eye on him. Plus, I need him to bring in his brother." He sends me a sidelong look. "Who just suddenly up and vanished."

"No," Sadie cuts in. "Colton can't be out there. For once, Carson's right. The UNSUB is using whatever and whoever to get to me. I can't chance Colton getting hurt."

Quinn runs a hand through his hair and groans. "It's the only way to cover every angle without giving up our leads." His gaze is hard on her, and I can see the understanding in her eyes as it hits.

Her connection to all of this is already in question. The less people who know about it, the better for her. "I'll go," I say. "I'll go wherever and do whatever if it helps. But I'm not being used to setup my brother." I give Carson a menacing glare.

Carson scoffs. "Still protecting him, huh?"

"You're a fucking idiot. You know that, right?" I step toward him, but Quinn pushes between us.

"Knock that shit off. We don't have time for vendettas, Carson. Just work the fucking leads." He slaps a packet against Carson's chest. "I want the surveillance at The Lair scoured. Anyone on those top levels that doesn't belong, that doesn't have access, I want that footage. And I want the whereabouts of those two members you flagged logged and questioned, Colton." He glances from me to Sadie. "Bonds said the UNSUB might've been at the club last night. Prove it. Get me a fucking clear image of this bastard."

"Detective Quinn?" Carson says, drawing Quinn's full attention. "I worked this case for a long time. I have suggestions on the profile that doesn't match with what Agent Bonds is suggesting."

Running a hand down his face, Quinn sighs. Then he waves his hand, prompting Carson on.

Carson straightens his back. "Agent Bonds wants to keep communication open with the UNSUB. But according to her own profile, this is feeding his narcissistic supply. It's empowering him. We should shut down all communication with him."

Sadie and I share a look. We know exactly what happens when the UNSUB loses contact with her, and right now—with Sadie's friend at his mercy; as much as I want to agree with Carson and stop this sick fuck from contacting Sadie—that can't happen.

"We can't get a trace on him, anyway," Carson continues. "He's only using it for recognition. He won't hurt Avery without an audience, right? And by supplying him with a direct link to this department, we're giving him that audience."

Sadie turns to Quinn, completely dismissing Carson. I let a smile slip.

"In theory, he's right. But in this instance? He's utterly wrong. The hostility the UNSUB exudes when he's ignored suggests he'll retaliate. He may have no plans to kill Avery...he could only want to bait me...but we could trigger an explosive reaction that endangers Avery if we kill communication."

With a nod, Quinn says, "I agree. We're not doing anything to jeopardize Avery."

Carson crosses his arms. "All right. Then me and rope boy are bringing in Julian as soon as possible. That's one way to knock a suspect off the list for sure."

My jaw ticks as I grit my teeth. This new desire to defend my brother is disturbing. I've spent so long loathing him; I feel I'm the only one allowed the right to make accusations against him.

"If that's the only way to eliminate him as a suspect," I say. "Then I'll find him. If he's here at the station, then he's not anywhere else."

A tight smile pulls at Sadie's lips. "Colton needs a phone. Something to stay in contact with us at all times since the techs confiscated his."

As Quinn beckons a tech over to get Sadie's request underway, I link my fingers through hers and pull her close. "This is for you," I whisper. "I don't give a damn about Julian."

She frowns. "I know. But clearing him will also clear any connection Carson is trying to pin on you." She kisses my cheek. The feel of her soft lips on my skin sparks a fiery pang in my chest.

"Promise me," I say to her.

Her features fall.

"Promise me you're only using it as a tactic. That you won't actually try to meet this sadistic fuck on your own."

With hesitation, she nods. "I promise that I won't...not right now. He's not falling for it anyway. There's too much coverage and surveillance. He can't chance giving himself away like this."

I release a breath. "Be safe."

"You, too. Anything you uncover, send it here. You and I will go over it."

Her implication is clear: we're the main targets, and we have to stay ahead of everyone else.

I turn toward Quinn with a warning ready on my tongue, but he says, "You don't have to say it. I won't let anything happen to her."

"I know." I stare him straight on, letting my eyes speak for me. *If anything happens to her, I'll end you.* Then I say to Carson, "Lead the way, detective."

He scoffs. "Fucking hell. If you end up being the UNSUB, I will kill you dead."

I raise my eyebrows at him. "Ditto."

PIECES

SADIE

Pressure builds behind my eyes, around my forehead, at my temples. It's the physical manifestation of the weight bearing down on me —the pressure to connect all the pieces and save Avery.

I glance down at my phone, check the time. I imagine I can hear the ticking of the clock counting down the hours. The minutes. The *seconds*. But it's all in my head. Right there with the mounting pressure.

I hit my office quickly to change into a pair of jeans and a T-shirt I had stashed there. Quinn thought it'd be a good idea to change, get comfortable for the long day ahead of us. It's almost as if I can't think for myself. I *hate* this feeling. Completely disoriented. It's like…if I can just uncover one clue, just pinpoint the abduction site, then I can connect the rest of this puzzle.

And so that's where we start. With the clock ticking, Quinn and I begin at the one place we know Avery always to be. Her lab.

"What is the last communication you had with her?" Quinn asks as he sets up the standing UV lamp. He brought his laptop with us and is conducting the search and comparison against the department while I attempt to determine the abduction site.

You would think that an M.E.'s lab—being equipped with every type of forensic equipment at the ready—would be the perfect environment to mount an investigation. It's the exact opposite, however. As Quinn switches on the lamp, the light illuminates a massive amount of substances. From the blood of previous victims, to every other conceivable body fluid.

I close my eyes for a second as the pressure nearly doubles me over.

Shaking off the forming headache, I say, "I spoke with her the night before last. Right here."

"About?" At my sigh, he adds, "Sadie. We have to do this. You know we have to go over every detail."

"I know." Taking a look around, I let my gaze scan the room, seeking anything out of place. It's like a clustered science fair maze. I was terrible at science. "I asked her for a favor. I needed a workup on some rope. She said she'd make it her first priority."

Quinn adjusts his forensic glasses. "A comparison for Colton. To clear him."

"Yes, Quinn. To clear him...or to damn him. I always pursue the truth."

"Hey," he says, pausing his task to meet my eyes. "I'm not judging you. I would've done the same in your position."

I let a wan smile steal across my face. "Anyway. I don't think she had time to look into it." I pull the letter from my back pocket. "Her assistant gave me this yesterday." I unfold the note. "Sadie, I'm sorry I wasn't able to complete your request. I've come down with something, but I promise to work on it as soon as possible. Trust your gut...until I can get you some answers. Avery."

"What time was the letter delivered to you? By who?"

"A lab tech...Simon. Right before I left the station yesterday morning." I press my fingers against the bridge of my nose. "Presumably, she wrote it the night before...or very early in the morning." I slip on a pair of glasses. "She did tell me she wasn't feeling well when we last spoke."

Quinn braces his hands behind his head, going into his deep thinking mode. "So she writes a note with instructions for it to get to you before she heads home. That doesn't sound like Avery. Even if she was ill, why not just call you?"

I shake my head. "She was working late that night. Maybe she left it at the lab because it was too late to call, and she didn't want to be bothered the next day."

"Why not text?"

I tilt my head. "What are you getting at? I can see Avery writing a letter. She's pretty old-school. Not more so than you, but she appreciates the simpler times." I inwardly smile, remembering her fussing over a computer error one day in the lab.

"All right," Quinn says. "If that checks out, then she had to be abducted shortly afterward. I think we should head to her house and help CSU conduct the search."

I scan the letter again, looking for any signs that she wrote it under duress. "I took her advice," I say as I spread the note out on the table. "She's the only one in her field who would ever say such a thing. 'Trust your gut.'" I shake my head and almost laugh. Then I glance at Quinn. "Well, maybe except for you."

He squeezes out a tight smile. "Forensics doesn't leave much in the way of trusting your instincts. It's all about the facts."

"Right. And she is the best." I angle the letter to catch the UV light. "If she was on to something, it makes sense the UNSUB would want to stop her. It's the only reason—other than to hurt me—I can think of as to why he took her."

The light sets off fingerprints—presumably Avery's—on the note. I take the bi-chromatic powder from my kit and dust the prints, then lift them carefully with tape.

"You really think he was bold enough to abduct her here rather than her home."

Placing the tape on a card, I mark the evidence and then repeat the process with another print. "Do I think he's bold enough? Yes. And it makes sense. He wanted me kept away from the department the night I watched over my mother. I thought then it was because he didn't want me to interfere with Colton's interrogation. But maybe it was more than that. Maybe he had Avery in his sights all along."

The truth of that kills. I should've warned her. How many people in my life is he planning to torture? With that thought comes an abundance of guilt. So much so that I'm having a difficult time taking in an even breath.

"I've put two of my best on keeping a lookout over your mother," Quinn says, as if he's mentally tapping into my thoughts. I'm probably completely transparent. Unable to mask anything at this point.

"Thank you." I swallow hard as I lift the last print. "I'm sure these are Avery's, but I don't want to leave any piece of evidence out of the investigation." I place the cards on Avery's worktable. "We should hurry. The techs need to get back in here so they can keep working on what Avery—"

I cut myself off as it comes to me. "What was Avery last working on? I mean, besides what I asked for." I look around, trying to deduce her methodology. It's tidy and neat…but in a way that probably only makes sense to Avery.

"The last time I heard from her, she called me about

the third vic. She was working on a physical profile of the UNSUB based on the strength needed to hoist a body. We planned to run through it with a computer program to simulate the crime scene."

Her computer.

Everyone in the lab has access to the same files, but Avery has her own, tightly guarded notes. I remove my glasses and pull up a chair, then tap the keyboard, awakening the screen.

While I log in under my ID and search through Avery's files, Quinn says, "She could've been abducted at any point from here to her home. So far, CSU hasn't uncovered anything at her house. We should broaden the search." He moves toward the wall lockers, inspecting the fingerprints. "Everyone has been in this lab at some point. If the UNSUB did find a way in here, it's like searching for a damn needle in a haystack for evidence."

"He's intelligent. He would've used forensic countermeasures to remove any evidence. But he's not perfect, Quinn. This abduction was hasty. If he was here, right under the department's nose, even someone with a god complex is cautious enough to be quick about it."

"For Avery's sake, I hope you're right." Quinn resumes his search.

"We know the UNSUB deviated greatly from his MO in order to abduct Avery," I say, flipping through each file on the victims. "We know the vic—" I break off, irritated with myself for referring to Avery as a victim. "We know the target personally this time. So he couldn't perform his ritual at her home. That changes everything. We have to come at this from a completely different angle. It has to have greater meaning for him in order for him to pull a switch at this point. And that means he still could've left us something either at her house, or here, or wherever he abducted her from. Something to mark his territory." I release a strenuous breath as I locate Avery's current notes on the third vic. "He's too vain to pass up an opportunity to show us how clever he is. He needs to brag."

"But if it was a spur of the moment attack rather than planned out, that could mean we're wasting our time looking for a clue," Quinn says. "Besides, there are no signs of a struggle here." Quinn turns around and focuses the light on the ceiling-mounted body hangers near the autopsy tables. "Wait."

I look up. Quinn tilts his head as he examines the white straps of one of the hangers with a gloved hands. "What is it?"

"I'm not sure." He motions me over. "Stand in front here."

I glance at the screen again before I meet him in the middle of the lab, where he positions me in front of the hanger.

"You're smaller than Avery, but it should still line up fairly the same." He raises my arms and mimics wrapping the strap around one of my wrists. "There's no need to restrain a body here…since they're all pretty compliant, considering they're dead."

"Not funny, Quinn."

"I'm not trying to be." His eyes meet mine. "The straps are twisted and look here—" he brings one forward and points to a tear. "I'm no lab tech, but I highly doubt anyone would need to secure a dead body this tightly in a hanger."

I glance around, frantic. "There." I point to a scalpel on the worktable. He grabs the tool and moves me in front of the second hanger. Before he even begins to reenact the scene, my heart is pounding in my ears.

"We'll try this out here so we don't add trace to the other hanger," he says as he secures my wrist with the strap.

A few weeks ago, this scenario would've decimated me. The feel of the strap tightening around my wrist floods me with panic, but it's not my fear. It's the realization that Avery experienced this—it's her terror leveling me, the dread of what she must've suffered.

Even still, the situation causes my arms to tremble. Quinn isn't Colton—the only man I've ever trusted to restrain me. As the straps begin to constrict my movement, I flinch away, knocking Quinn's chin with my elbow.

He groans and backs away, cupping his jaw.

"Oh, shit—sorry."

He curses and works out his jaw. "Nice elbow, Bonds. Right in my tooth."

"Jesus, Quinn. You still haven't seen a dentist?"

He shakes off the pain and rights himself. "With what time?" A determined glint lights his eyes as he steps closer. "Try not to punch me, okay?" He finishes tying off the straps, then looks over the restraints. "This isn't right."

He drops his hands with a huff. "Avery's a fighter. She would've screamed. She would've struggled, not stood here like this, just letting him tie her up."

"She was drugged," I say, envisioning the scene. "Like I said, he had to veer from his MO. If she was sedated, he could easily subdue her."

Quinn must agree, because he moves behind me and wraps his arm around my waist. "He'd have to hold her in place." I let my body go lax, trying and failing not to picture Avery in my place. I shut my eyes. Breathe through the horror of it.

As he gets my other wrist bound, he grunts as he reaches for one of the scalpels on the table. He pushes the tool through the strap, securing it closely against my wrist. He does the same thing to my other arm. His hard chest holds me up as I lean against him. He turns one of my wrists toward him. "The size of the hole in the strap matches. The UNSUB restrained her right in her own lab, the motherfucker. How did CSU miss this?"

"That's a good question," I say, wriggling my wrist free. "But there's an even more obvious one we need to be asking." I free my other wrist and start toward the computer. "The UNSUB is meticulous. Everything planned, every detail covered. But instead of using his own tools, restraining her with his own rope, he used what was handy to him at the time."

Quinn's face contorts in a stern frown. "As if he was already close. Already in the building. And abducting Avery *was* a spur of the moment choice. Dammit."

"Exactly." I tap the mouse pad and open Avery's most recent file. "And, instead of abducting her quickly, he restrained her here. There was something here he wanted."

He removes his glasses. "You were right, Bonds. Avery was on to something. She was in his way." Quinn paces the length of the room as he takes out his phone and calls in the update. "We need to block off the M.E. lab. Get this place yellow taped and order in a full sweep. This time, focusing on a captive situation."

As he ends the call, I look up and say, "Quinn, I don't trust anyone to go through the evidence here. We need to figure out what's missing—if anything—before the team comes in for another sweep."

"Hell. That could take damn near all day, if not longer." He moves to stand beside me and points to the screen. "What were her last notes?"

I shake my head. "You said she was going to work with you on the third vic scenario. But her recent entry is on the last vic. Her theories and tests on exsanguination." I run through her notes, looking at the timestamps. "Shit."

Quinn catches on quickly. "He deleted files."

"We need a tech to go through the metadata."

Quinn turns the keyboard toward him. "No time." He

scans the evidence logs, looking for anything checked out by Avery. When that doesn't produce results, he clicks open the server and proceeds to pull up logs for the past two days.

"How do you know how to do this? You're the last person I'd assume to be computer savvy."

A smile twitches at his mouth. "I'm full of surprises, Bonds." He looks over and winks before returning to his search. "Bingo. It's not a full record, but it's enough. Her last entry was on evidence identifier three-oh-one." He pulls up the chain of custody files and locates the item information. "The rope recovered at the third crime scene on the suspended vic."

I'm out of the seat and searching the evidence lockers for the rope.

Quinn puts in a call to the evidence room in the station. "Who signed it out? When?" His gaze follows me around the room. "Okay, thanks."

"Let me guess. It was already signed out by Avery," I say, shutting the locker.

"Yeah."

"The rope isn't here. Neither is the sample I gave her." I press my hands to my forehead, trying to push away the growing ache. "Avery had him. She found his mistake. She had to—and it cost her." I steeple my fingers over my mouth, thinking. "Who else would have access to her notes? The whole lab? Someone else has to know what she found."

"Kyle has every lab tech up in holding taking statements."

"We need to be ahead of this. We have to consider the possibility that—"

"I know, Sadie." Quinn shoves a hand through his hair. His phone beeps, and he looks down at the message. "Damn. Kyle says one tech didn't come in today. It was reported to be her day off, but no one can get ahold of her."

"She could know what Avery discovered." A sinking feeling pulls at my stomach. "She could also be the leak, Quinn."

"Maybe." Quinn grabs an evidence bag and drops the scalpel inside. "Let's secure the scene, then we're heading to that tech. She can't come in to make a statement, we'll go to her."

I nod and quickly mark the hanger, shoving my fears aside. My hands suffer a sudden tremor, and I drop the roll of evidence tape. "Crap." I watch it roll under Avery's desk. Crouching down, I reach for the roll and spot something on the underside of the desk.

"Oh, my god. Avery, you're so sneaky." I reach up and detach a notebook from the desk.

Quinn walks over. "You got trace?"

I smile up at him. "Better." Dropping the book into a bag, I say, "We got Avery's personal notes. Old-school style."

He lends me a hand, helping me to my feet, then taps

his phone. "Kyle, forward me all the statements of the lab techs and have the analysts go through the lab surveillance and the servers. Someone deleted files. I want to know why and how it was missed, and how someone got into the system. See if there's any altered surveillance and keep me updated."

"You didn't tell him about the missing evidence."

He drops his phone into his trench coat pocket and guides me toward the double doors. "That's because I don't want the lab techs to know what we know yet."

"You don't trust Kyle?" I ask as I grab my bag before we push through the doors.

"I don't trust anyone anymore."

A heaviness weighs on my chest. I've lived with that mistrust my whole life—and now it's returned with a vengeance.

FRAILTY

COLTON

"**Y**ou scored big."

I ignore Carson's comment and instead check my phone. Sadie had one of the computer guys at the station install GPS software on our phones so we can locate the other quickly.

Right now, she's still at the department. As long as that little green dot on my screen stays active, I'm able to breathe. And to put up with Carson's shit. He hasn't stopped talking since we got in the car.

"I mean, a member of the ACPD. A profiler, no doubt." Carson glances over at me, a smug smile stretching his face. "That's a pretty worthy notch. Makes you look real good. Hell, and it's Sadie. Tight little ass. Nice, perky tits. The other officers will probably take it easy on you just for the fact that you got in her pants, man. Not that she hasn't been around. But that's just inner office gossip." He sends me another smile. "You know that, right?"

Normally, I'd have him jacked up against his seat and on his way out the car door for talking about her that way, but I'm letting his bullshit roll right off. I get it—the petty attempt to rile me, to trip me up. I'm just offended he thinks I'm simple enough to fall for some cliché detective shit.

He pulls into a spot in front of The Lair. Turns toward me as he opens his door. "Of course, not all the rumors are that far off. You know how freaky she is. It's kind of obvious why Quinn has me babysitting you. Keeping you away from Sadie so he can have her to himself."

Still, I'm not above jealousy when it comes to Sadie. Carson is probing for a weak spot. And when my grip tightens on the phone, he chuckles.

"For Sadie's sake, and what she's going through right now..." I say as I get out of the car and look at him from across the roof. "I'm not going to give you what you want. We can spend all day taking jabs at each other. Or we can work together."

His eyes squint. "We're not partners. We're not working together, *dude*. You're a fucking suspect in a criminal investigation, and your brother—and this club—is in the middle of all of it."

I shrug. "Even so, you need my *cooperation*." I slam

the door shut. "You need a lot more from me than I do from you, rook. Trying to push my buttons so I take a swing at you and get locked up for the day? Not happening. Though, I would really love to put my fist through your face." I smile. "Rain check?"

He flips me off.

As we head to the front door, I pull my key ring out and Carson straightens his tie. "Just get your brother here. That's all the cooperation I need from you."

That tick in my eye has Carson's name on it. As soon as this is over...

My train of thought veers off as I nudge the door and it cracks open. Carson already has his gun drawn as he pushes me aside and takes up the front.

"Stay here," he says, knocking the door open with his foot. He quickly checks all angles before he moves into the club.

Watching him is like watching a cop show. For all of Carson's douchery, he takes charge like a true cop. But I'm not one to hang back. I follow his lead, checking the hallway entrance twice, before I enter the main level.

"I should have a gun," I say as I look for anything out of place. This could've been a break-in, but what kind of person needs to rob a BDSM club? I can't imagine anyone being that hard up.

Carson called it when he said the club is at the center of all this. I know my role, why the UNSUB has it out for me, but there's got to be more. Which really has me questioning what my brother's part is. Julian has to play some role of his own. I need to get a handle on that before Carson does.

When Carson feels the bottom level is clear, he lowers his gun. "The last thing I'm doing is giving you a gun." He shakes his head. "You're a fucking suspect. Do you not get that?"

"Yeah, I get that. But according to Sadie's profile, so is everyone at the department. That includes you, Detective Dick." He starts toward me, but I keep moving toward the stairs. Every second wasted fighting with Carson is a second keeping me away from Sadie. "Let's check the surveillance. It doesn't look like whoever was here stole anything. Nothing's wrecked or damaged. Doubt it's vandalism."

He laughs. "Now you're a detective? Why don't you stick with the pervy shit and leave the detecting to me."

I start to lead the way up the spiral staircase, but Carson jumps ahead. Fine by me. He can take the bullet.

Once we reach the top level, I find the office door unlocked and open. A sick feeling worms its way into my stomach as I enter. Nothing looks touched, but there's an eerie feeling floating through the room, as if someone was just here.

"Pull up the surveillance," Carson says. He sinks into one of the cushioned chairs, but keeps his gun at the ready.

I take a seat behind the desk. "We're not partners,

remember? And I sure as hell don't work for you. So don't bark orders at me."

He smiles and bats his eyes. "Pretty please?"

I punch my password in and glance up. "What is your issue with me? Just because you think you have some evidence…that proves what? That I know my rope?"

His brow furrows. "My gut instinct says you're involved."

I guess I can't argue with that. I'm not exactly innocent. But I keep Sadie's words from last night close. She's all the exoneration I need.

"It's up," I say. Carson moves to stand beside me as I launch the playback footage of last night. "I should check the log of the break-in first."

He pulls up a chair. "Keep rolling last night's footage. Finding the UNSUB is more important than your insurance claim right now."

I hate this guy—but he's right. The sooner we can discover the identity of the UNSUB, the sooner Sadie is out of harm's way.

Carson looses a heavy breath. "Damn. This is going to take hours. Skip ahead to the timeframe where the UNSUB sent a pic of Sadie to your phone."

He doesn't know all the details, but he knows just enough to make me uncomfortable. The letter the UNSUB pushed under my door last night feels heavy in my pocket. It's too damn close to him right now.

I move the footage up to later in the night…and spot

Sadie. Sitting at her table, just like the image of her on my phone. I try to remember the angle of the pic. *Where is he?* My eyes scan the edges of the room, the stage, the bar… and then the screen goes black.

"What the fuck?" Carson says.

My sentiment exactly. I tap the keyboard, trying to figure out the glitch. But my gut says this is no malfunction. "It's gone. Deleted."

"Sonofabitch." Carson slams his hand on the desk. He whips out his phone. "Quinn, we have a problem. The security files at the club have been tampered with. Some footage from last night is missing." A beat. "All right. I'll keep you posted."

He ends the call and says to me, "Make a copy. I'm getting a uni to deliver the original to the techs at the department. They might be able to recover the deleted footage. We'll keep watching the rest to log any suspects."

And so that's what we do. We settle in for the long haul. With hours and hours of surveillance footage to watch, and my goddess too far away.

My eyes feel like they're bleeding. Carson isn't fairing any better.

"I thought this would be awesome," he says, rubbing

his temples. "Hot Dominatrixes working guys over. Nasty sex kittens getting it on with each other… But I gotta tell you, I think I'm scarred for life." He blinks hard at the screen. "There is such a thing as too much porn."

I exhale heavily. "It's not porn. No sex happens on the floor."

"And off the floor?"

I grit my teeth.

"Whatever," he says. "You know what I mean. Too much of a freaky thing is just too much of a freaky thing." He checks the time on his phone. "Why isn't your brother returning your calls?"

"He's recently engaged. I'm sure his fiancé is keeping him busy." *Or he left.* Sadie's call to him to obtain a lawyer for me probably scared him off. Julian's already been through one investigation with Carson; he won't stick around for another.

"You want to know what I think?" Carson says, propping his booted feet up on the desk. I crane an eyebrow, annoyed. "There was no forced entry. Someone with a key walked right into this club and deleted surveillance files. And now, that someone is nowhere to be found."

As much as I loathe the guy, he has a point. Julian and I are the only ones with keys to the club. Since I was with Sadie at the department this morning, that leaves the question of my brother. But why? Not to protect me, that's for sure. And doing something so obvious only implicates him further. There has to be another reason, like high profile members being on those surveillance files. Maybe he's trying to protect his cash cows.

Or... "Someone could've stolen his key," I say, a sudden fear washing over me. The UNSUB got to me easily; he could've just as easily gotten to Julian.

Carson sinks his chin on his hand, his eyes looking glazed and far away as he considers this possibility. "We need to go." He leaps up, already grabbing his jacket.

"I'm not going anywhere. I'm sticking right here and finding this son of a bitch on this footage. He's here somewhere, and I'm going to match him to Sadie's profile."

"Profile," he mocks. "I spent time at Quantico. I can tell you the fucking basics of a serial killer, too. And I can tell you he's not on that footage. He's smart enough to have us chasing our tails for weeks. You think he's just going to pop up on the screen? We're wasting our time here. Besides, the techs are going over the surveillance. They'll find something before we do."

"I'm not here for you. I'm here for Sadie. This is how she feels I can help, so it's where I'm focusing."

He smirks. "Man, she has you whipped. Not hard to figure out who's the dominant in your relationship."

Fire simmers beneath my skin. "I'm not ashamed to admit I serve her. Worship her. If you think you're insulting me, you're wrong. I'll always obey her orders."

His forehead creases. Then he turns to go. "Fucking freaky shit…" he says under his breath.

"Good luck trying to find Julian on your own." I have a good idea where my brother took off to, but I'm not letting Carson bring him in without me.

Carson reaches for the doorknob right as the door opens. He steps back as a man in a black trench coat enters. "Who the fuck are you?"

The guy—his face impassive at Carson's remark—flashes an ID badge. "FBI. Special Agent Proctor."

"Fucking hell," Carson says.

I glance at the monitors. Four other FBI agents are on the main level overturning furniture. Shit. I let Carson distract me and didn't even see them enter.

I stand. "You can't be in here without a—"

"Warrant?" Agent Proctor interrupts. He slaps a folded paper against my chest as he passes. "We're now heading up this investigation. Everything in this club is considered evidence."

I scan the warrant. I'm not sure what I'm looking for, but it seems legit. Carson snatches it out of my hands and looks it over. "You can't just come in and take over. We've been working this case since the beginning. Who called you in?"

Leaning over the desk, Proctor eyes the computer screen. "You know how this works, detective. The FBI has jurisdiction in any city. Let's try to work together on this. There's no call to start a pissing contest." He glances up at

Carson. "You have two options. Work with the FBI to bring in the perp, or use your sick days to take a vacation. Your choice."

Arms crossed, Carson matches the agent's stern glare. "I don't take sick days."

"Good," Proctor says. "Your department is being briefed right now. You should probably check in there to get your new assignment, detective."

Carson's jaw ticks. As the agent pulls my chair up to the desk and starts scanning the surveillance files, Carson cocks his head toward the door. I follow him into the hallway.

"You have anything incriminating on that computer?" he asks me.

"You're not using this to interrogate me. I told you. I have nothing to hide." Which is true. There's nothing on that computer or in this club that should set off red flags to the Feds. Even Julian's stash under the floorboard shouldn't raise too many questions. It's all just memorabilia of the investigation into Marni—which I'm sure the FBI already knows everything about.

The club has plenty of higher-ups as members—the ACPD captain, for one—but those files aren't located on the system. They're safely hidden in Sadie's car.

There's still a thick feeling of dread coming over me, however. Having the FBI in my club isn't good. Not at all. If they deem, they can shut it down until this investigation ends, and the only place we know for sure that the UNSUB has been is in this club. Right now, Carson is more of a comrade than these agents. That's a fucked up thought.

"You have the addresses of those two suspect members?" Carson asks.

I nod. "It's better to bring them here rather than go knocking on doors, though. Don't you think?"

His face hardens. "Yeah. That was the plan before the damn turf invaders showed up. You think anyone's going to want to come here tonight with the black coats skulking about?"

He just voiced my fear. "Looks like you're getting your way, Carson." At his confused expression, I say, "We're going to my brother."

PULSE

SADIE

We have been invaded.

The stench of leather and fast food and cheap coffee saturates the air of the ACPD. It's a nauseating smell that seeps past my practicality and triggers my defenses.

The FBI blew in like a hurricane, sweeping the task force up into a funnel of federal ordinances and churning out a well-oiled, bureaucratic command post.

We should've known it would come to this. With the extensive news coverage on the killings, and now the abduction of a medical examiner, it was inevitable. Actually, I'm surprised it's taken as long as it has for the Feds to intervene…or interfere, as that's how Quinn is seeing this new directive.

Amid the functioning hub of the task force, a showdown is looming. I stealthily slip Quinn's laptop into my bag as he marches toward the special agent dictating the operations.

"Get your lead agent here *now*!" Quinn shouts. This agent must've drawn the short straw when they were deciding who would inform Quinn of the takeover.

The agent holds his place. "I'm Special Agent Rollins. Agent Proctor will be here directly. Until then, I have all the specifics to fill you in, Detective Quinn."

Recognition lights Quinn's eyes right before his gaze sharpens on Agent Rollins. "Proctor sent me a fucking proxy?" He laughs mockingly. "I want to see him. Right now. Get that smug SOB here or—"

"Detective Quinn," Wexler interrupts. Startled, I turn to see our captain standing fists to hips in his office door. "My office. You, too, Agent Bonds."

I know what's coming. Quinn can roar and stomp his feet all he wants, but when the Feds come in, it's game over for the local guys. For once, I know how Quinn must've felt the times I got assigned to his cases when I was with the General Investigation Section.

Wexler closes the door behind us.

"Captain, you know what this means—"

"Save it, Quinn. Maybe if this were any other case, we'd get into a jurisdictional pissing war with the Feds, but not now. Not with our M.E.'s life on the line." He crosses his arms. "I'm the one who brought them in."

Betrayal colors Quinn's face, and I feel the resounding burn.

Wexler rubs the back of his neck and sighs. "Nothing changes. You and Sadie keep the task force on point. But let the Feds take the reins."

A muscle feathers along Quinn's jaw. "This is a slap in the face, Captain."

"No, it's an order." Wexler holds Quinn's gaze a second longer before he looks at me. "Agent Bonds doesn't seem to have an issue. Do you?"

I press my lips together as I try to subdue my anger. It doesn't work. "Actually, I do." Quinn turns my way, eyebrows reaching toward his hairline. "The FBI's main focus will be on apprehending the UNSUB—not on bringing Avery back alive. I take every offense to this method. Especially since Quinn and I weren't informed beforehand."

Wexler releases another heavy breath. "Point taken. But that's where I'm depending on you two. Let the Feds have the glory of capturing the bad guy. You two make sure Avery stays safe. That's it. Not another word. Dismissed."

As Quinn and I leave Wexler's office, he says to me, "This feels like some bureaucratic bullshit. Something tells me this wasn't Wexler's call at all."

"Possibly," I say. "And I don't like it any more than you do, for Avery's sake...but regardless, he's right, Quinn."

"How?"

"Because, now we can put our full attention on tracking down Avery. Let the Feds investigate the UNSUB. They can bring him down, dead or alive. I don't care how or with what means."

"You sure about that?" He glances over at me, concern etched on his features.

No. Not at all. The FBI will scrutinize every detail about Lyle Connelly. Which will inevitably link back to me. But I already decided to face my consequences when this ends. As long as it ends with Avery alive and safe, it will be worth the sacrifice.

"Let's just get back to work," I say. "Every fucking second that we deal with some setback, that's another second Avery suffers."

As Quinn addresses Kyle, his first in command on the task force, I give Agent Rollins the update on the profile. His keen observation about the connection between the Roanoke killings and the current killing spree puts me on edge. Obviously, the Feds have been conducting their own investigation. Whereas they now have access to all our data, we don't have any insight into theirs.

That barrier presents a blind spot I can't see around.

I've lost the advantage to anticipate what's coming.

As we start out of the bullpen, I'm impressed with Quinn's ability to suppress his urge to punch one of the agents going through his office.

I can hear the restraint in his voice. "What's your

thoughts on how the UNSUB will handle the FBI taking over?"

"Honestly. He'll enjoy the attention. This might actually buy Avery more time." The downside? If the FBI decides to seize communication with the UNSUB. That could trigger a volatile reaction.

I clutch my phone, reassured by the fact that the Feds didn't confiscate it or the burner in my pocket. I'm sure that's coming, but right now, I have two communication links to Avery. Two lifelines that the FBI will have to pry out of my hands before I give them up.

Quinn knocks on the door for a second time. "You sure this is the right address?"

I check Carmen Moore's info on my phone. "It was logged by Avery herself. She keeps tight records." Even in her personal, handwritten notes.

On the way here, I read through her journal. Her last log was on the missing evidence—the rope from the suspended vic crime scene. She noted the discovery of epithelial cells within the fiber. Possible DNA from the perpetrator.

In her mention, she theorized that although the offender wore gloves (the presence of synthetic polymers were also found on the rope), if he had wrapped the rope around his arm to hoist the body, the rope could've picked up transfer skin cells.

It's such a simple, logical but ultimately brilliant finding.

My only misgiving is accepting that the UNSUB would make such an obvious oversight.

But everyone—no matter how well they plan—makes a mistake eventually.

The computer analyst confirmed that it was the last entry made on her computer. That coupled with the call she made to Quinn shortly after, requesting his help with building a physical profile of the UNSUB with a simulation, gives us a close approximation of the abduction time.

At 10:35 PM, Avery's file was deleted from her computer.

Quinn has the task force techs trying to recover surveillance footage of the M.E. lab from that night. Our mission: to investigate if the missing lab tech knows about the discovery of the epithelial cells.

"Avery had to create a sample when she found the skin cells," I say, anxiousness clawing at me.

Quinn adjusts his stance, his growing impatience as evident as mine. "If she had, why wouldn't she run it through CODIS?"

"Maybe she didn't have time." Or maybe she did run it through the database and got a hit on someone within the department. It's possible that's why she called Quinn to meet her the next day, feeling unable or unsafe to mention her findings over the phone.

I run my hand over my face, as if I can physically organize my wandering thoughts into a straight timeline. I'm making leaps without facts; we need this tech to have the answers.

I angle my phone away from Quinn and toggle to the GPS app. Colton and Carson are on the move away from The Lair. Knowing that Special Agent Proctor and his team infiltrated the club, I'm relieved. I send Colton a quick update, then close the screen.

"How do you know Proctor?" I ask.

Rolling his shoulders, Quinn works out his neck. "I don't. Not really. But he's stepped on my toes before on a couple of cases in the past." He raises his hand to knock, then changes his mind and rings the doorbell. "You surprised me back there."

"How?"

"I figured you'd be all about the FBI coming in. Isn't Quantico like, the profiler mother planet?"

I bite down on my lip. "With my past cases—" I avoid his eyes "—I don't want the FBI looking too closely." And there it is. The reason why I never applied to the FBI. Now Quinn's question—the one he's wondered since I first transferred to the ACPD—has been answered.

He gives me a sideways look, his gaze probing. But he

doesn't push. It's safer to leave things unsaid until we reach that point of no return.

It will come soon enough.

Quinn checks the handle and it turns. He glances at me. "It's open."

I have the sudden impulse to remark on Quinn disregarding his own by-the-book protocol, but I resist the urge. If the lab tech who lives here has the information we need to help Avery, I will back him one-hundred-percent on breaking all the rules.

I follow Quinn inside the foyer. The sound of loud voices comes from the direction of the living room, and Quinn places his hand on his piece inside his coat.

"Carmen," he shouts. "It's Detective Quinn with the ACPD." He nods to the hallway as he continues toward the living room. "I'm here to ask you some questions. Are you home?"

I check the short hall, nodding once to let him know it's clear.

"We need your help in a matter involving—" He breaks off at the sight of the woman sprawled on the floor. "Sadie, radio in a bus."

The amount of red soaking the gray carpet around her head gives me pause, just for a second, before I unclip my radio. I fumble with the hem of my shirt, using it to grab the remote on a table and mute the TV, then radio for an ambulance.

"Be careful of the blood pool," I say as Quinn kneels

beside her. He reaches into his pocket and yanks out a glove, using it as a barrier between himself and the blood coating her neck.

"I got a pulse. But it's weak. She's unresponsive." He stands and looks over the scene. "Jesus."

I get closer to inspect. The laceration on her neck is severe, but the carotid was missed. On purpose? The UNSUB wouldn't make this mistake, unless he wanted her to bleed out slowly. Only...why? It doesn't work for me.

As Quinn locates a hand towel from the kitchen to staunch the bleeding, I calm my racing heart enough to examine the scene: her pants are unzipped and pushed down around her calves, but her underwear is in place. Not torn or stretched. Her chest is bare, and her wrists are bound with rope and pulled up over her head. But her skin is clear of marks. No contusions or cuts. No burns. No wax. Other than her arms being bound during the attack, there's no evidence that she was tortured beforehand.

I remove a pen from my notebook and lift the hem of her jeans. There's no discerning ligature marks. Her ankles weren't bound. This whole attack feels...off.

"This was a hasty job," Quinn says, echoing my thoughts as he applies pressure to the wound.

I point to her neck. "But he didn't complete it. He doesn't leave his victims alive, Quinn."

Quinn shakes his head. "He could've been rushed. Something interrupted him. Or he knew he didn't have enough time."

I nod my agreement, but I'm not convinced. Why start if he knew he couldn't finish? That's not his MO. The UNSUB stalks his prey for days, even months beforehand. He has their schedules memorized, knows all the important details of their life to plan a methodical attack that will give him plenty of time to stage his scene.

For him, orchestrating the kill is just as important as the kill itself. It's his signature—torture. If he can't bring his victim to the brink, revel in his power, instilling her with fear…then there's no admiration for his efforts.

And he needs the admiration.

The second crime scene stated a blitz attack, where the UNSUB was rushed and infuriated when the vic fought back…but he made sure to complete his kill, even if he couldn't perform his ritual. If the case were similar here, Carmen would've suffered greatly. The torture would've been evident.

And the kill method… The UNSUB has enough training in forensics and medicine—either self taught or schooled—to know exactly how to sever an artery to perfectly direct the spray to lead us to a clue, but he misses on accident this time?

There's no logical reason as to why he'd leave a victim —a *witness*—alive.

Quinn picks up on my line of thought. "She might've seen his face, or some other defining characteristic. We have a witness."

"There's a reason why he wanted her silenced," I say,

looking at Quinn. "She's more than a witness. She's a clue."

As the EMTs load Carmen onto a gurney and hurry her into the ambulance, I can't stop going over it in my head. No forced entry—just like with the other vics. The attack is similar enough; the MO seems to be the same, excluding the torture. With the amount of blood, it was difficult to tell, but I could determine a waved pattern to the laceration.

God, Avery… She would be able to deduce so much with just one look, where I'm only guessing. I'm trying hard to trust my instincts, but I'm not Quinn, either. I don't operate purely on my gut. I need more facts.

My thoughts halt as I feel a hand on my shoulder. "We should follow them in," Quinn says. "Soon as she comes around, we need to be there to take her statement."

I move out of his touch, glancing around the house, needing something…else. Something more as to why the UNSUB chose her. What did he leave behind? Where's the damn connection to Bathory?

"Sadie?"

I find Quinn's gaze. "Okay. Let's hope she recovers soon."

His gaze narrows as he studies me a moment longer. I pull my wall into place. Quinn's not getting past it this time. There's too much unknown…and I have more than myself to keep protected.

While Quinn secures the crime scene, I take another

look around Carmen's living room. My gaze is drawn to the rich blood pool. So thick it's the darkest shade of crimson. Did he hold her in place while she bled out? How long did he watch the red flow? Was he so mesmerized by the life fading away slowly in her eyes that he couldn't bring himself to end her quickly?

I know what it's like. The first time you see real, violent blood. The life-force of it, the power. I understand how intoxicating the draw to analyze it is—to try to comprehend it's meaning when you first feel it...

I walk over and inspect the pool. There it is. One shade lighter than the rest. A clear impression. A slight touch of the hand to sample the kill.

Only someone taking a life for the first time would be this riveted, this careless.

And he's not the UNSUB.

ME

UNSUB

I f one is to understand himself, one must consider the nature, that is, the essence of humankind in general. It's an undertaking into the study of philosophical anthropology. Granted, I've earned a degree in order to work among peers in my field, to earn a living —but it was merely a requirement, a burden placed upon me by society.

I pride myself in the fact that I'm an autodidact, and have amassed most of my knowledge and mastery in the human condition through years of arduous study and research.

I've analyzed myself as much as I've placed others under the microscope.

And what I've discovered is that people—as a whole—are easily manipulated.

We yearn so desperately to make a connection, to know that we are not alone, that there is another in this world who feels what we feel. Who thinks how we think. Who accepts us wholly, unconditionally, and whom we can build companionship with so that we do not suffer this lonely existence in solitude, that we will do almost anything—*anything*—to avoid it.

When you understand that fundamental necessity, then it's only a matter of pulling the right strings—the heartstrings.

The most difficult moment of my study was in realizing that I'm not above this human condition, this affliction. However, there is liberation in stripping ones self of all misconceptions and lies to find true self discovery. It's a painful process, but then pain, as I've come to realize, is the purest method.

Most seek to ignore this yearning. They don't want to admit they are weak, would rather live in denial and leech off others to feed their needs. It's a selfish way to exist. And ultimately, we are a selfish species.

Why is it so difficult to admit our limitations, and in turn, strive to fulfill our desires? At any cost? Is there ever too high a price for absolute ecstasy?

After all, by doing so, we gain strength. He who controls his world commands the weak souls around him.

And every fucking one of them is weak.

I run the cane across Avery's back, reveling in the tremble of her racked body. She's hardly a weakling; so full of vibrant rebellion when she first arrived. But the beauty in understanding the human condition is in knowing how to break that character.

It's all just a matter of time and pressure. Much like with a rock. Water cascades over the rock, weathering away the stone, sending tiny fragments downstream as they break further apart. Just like that process, people can be eroded.

Leaning in close, I whisper, "Let's give our Sadie a show, shall we?"

She flinches, making the chains above rattle. Even now, after hours of weathering her stone surface away, she still believes in the lie. That she is strong enough on her own to overcome any hardship.

She's fighting against the current, her own nature, but she can only withstand so much force before she breaks. It's just a matter of time and pressure.

I wrap my arms around her tenderly as I twirl her to face the camera. Giving her what she so stubbornly denies she needs: connection.

"We must keep the world updated," I say, sliding the tip of the cane up her thigh. "Their utterly boring lives are invested in us. We should always please our audience. And Sadie needs this, even more than you do."

Oh, Sadie needs it terribly. She's like a diamond—hardest substance in the world. Chipping away Sadie's stone surface will take far less time with the help of breaking Avery.

It will send my love to her knees…then right into my arms.

Where she belongs.

A smile pulls at my mouth as I raise the cane, and I can't help but look directly into the camera lens. As if Sadie is watching me right now. Me. Her inevitability.

Avery's feet kick, trying to find purchase to push her away. Her cries swell into a forlorn tune, reaching only my ears. I brace my arm, but her sweet screams fade into the background as I pick up on the newscast. Annoyed, I turn toward the overhead screen.

A reporter stands before the hospital, giving viewers an update on the Arlington Slasher case, as a woman is wheeled in through the front doors on a gurney. Unable to reveal the victim's identity, the reporter does say the victim is a survivor of what's believed to be a related attack connected to the spree of serial killings.

Red covers my vision. Pulsing, blinding. A pure bolt of anger fires through my veins, and white-hot fury scorches my blood. In a moment of uncontrollable rage, I release a roar, choking the room of sound. A crackle fills my ears, then a deafening ringing.

I feel something warm trickle over my knuckles. I look down, see the cane splintered and my blood dripping to the plastic-covered floor. Little dots of bright red, mocking me.

I crick my neck, turning to face my pet. Avery's eyes—those orbs of chocolate brown—have become as pale as her ashen skin. Her fear tickles my senses, and I inhale the scent of urine. It streams down her leg.

That almost makes up for that amateur's fuck-up. Almost.

As always, I think as I slink toward my shivering pet, if you want something done right, you have to do it yourself. Time's run out. The tick tock of the clock just stopped for that one weak soul.

"Brace yourself, pet," I whisper into her ear. "It's time for your transformation into a Monarch."

I smile into the camera as Avery's screams drown my disappointment.

SHADOW

COLTON

When we were kids, Julian had a hiding spot in the woods. Whenever he'd get caught cheating on a test, or brought home a failing grade, or raised some other discontent he didn't want to deal with, he'd hide out in his fort until our parents were out of their minds with worry. Then he'd stumble in, dehydrated and filthy, and they were just so happy he was home that all was forgotten.

My brother is the quintessential Machiavellian. His manipulative behavior hasn't changed any over the years. Whenever he runs into an uncomfortable situation that he doesn't want to confront, he finds refuge in his hiding place until it's safe to show his face again.

Only now, instead of a child's hand-built fort, Julian boasts a two-story log cabin along the Potomac River.

"How do you know he's here?" Carson asks, shutting the door to his Crown Vic.

I enter in a code on the gate, and the wrought iron bars grind and screech open. "Because," I say, walking through to the pebbled driveway, "he's not answering my calls. He's off the grid."

"If he doesn't want to be found, wouldn't he go somewhere that you don't know about?"

I shrug. "I don't come here." In other words, I don't chase after my brother.

Julian and I have an understanding on that. Just like I knew to leave him alone during his funks when we were kids, he knows not to push my buttons. We're good at giving each other a wide berth, and plenty of space when we need it.

Except for now. I'm breaking that unspoken rule between us. All bets are off when it comes to Sadie.

"This place wasn't listed on any of Julian's financial reports." Carson's expression darkens as he takes in the sweeping terrace overlooking the river. "Can't see how I could've missed *this*."

"Not all detectives are cut out for the job." I cut a sharp glance his way, and he returns my glare. Truth is, this place wouldn't be on any financial statement. This is what a whole lot of bribery and cash under the table gets you.

Carson smirks. "Looks like the perfect place to

conduct sordid affairs…of the kidnapping and torture kind."

My smile drops. I march up the stairs toward the entrance, wanting to get this part over with. My brother might be a lot of questionable things, but a serial killer isn't one of them.

The sooner I prove that to Carson, the sooner I get back to Sadie. Her last update has me on edge. I can feel her panic and desperation in every message, and even though she's strong, I know everyone has a breaking point. I never want to see hers.

I don't knock. I go right through the front door, tripping the alarm. To the right, a panel flashes red. Carson radios in some report about the alarm, while I stare at the panel, trying to get inside my brother's degenerate head.

A painful ache twinges beneath my rib cage as it comes to me. Steadying my hand, I enter in Marni's birthday on the keypad. The alarm shuts off.

"I thought you never came here," Carson says.

He doesn't get a response on this one. When he had me in that interrogation room, dredging up painful memories of Marni, reminding me of choices I can never take back— I was there. At *my* breaking point. I won't give him any more ammunition.

"You'd think a loud-ass alarm system would alert the dead," he says, glancing around. "Your brother is either a heavy sleeper, piss drunk, or not here." He stops at the end of the foyer, turns around. "Unless he's somewhere else on the property. Like a basement…or a torture chamber. A nice, isolated spot where he can muffle the screams of tortured women."

I reach into my pocket and grip my rope. Needing just one measure of restraint to ground me. I close my eyes, breathe, open them. More in control.

Julian's seen my calls coming through. He knows I'm on the hunt for him, and I'm sure he knows it was me who tripped the alarm. I'm the only one who could've guessed that code. *Where the fuck is he?*

I take off up the stairs with Carson close on my heels. If Julian isn't here, then that means he's in deeper trouble than I thought. Our conversation about him wanting me to take over the club comes back to me. I honestly believed him—that he was giving up the lifestyle to get married.

I should've known better. Julian's too selfish to give anything up for another person.

He's hiding. But I don't know from whom or what. Who has he pissed off? Which one of his cash cows got tired of being blackmailed?

Even all these years later, after learning his tricks, he's still able to play me.

The second story of the cabin is one large, open loft. Equipped with just about every electronic, a gaming section with a pool table, and a playroom in the far corner, it's the ultimate man cave. That is, if your ideal haven includes bondage. I doubt his fiancé has ever been here— this is Julian's secret. Even—or especially—from her.

As Carson checks out the wall of bondage gear, I head toward Julian's computer area. "I'm calling in a sweep," he says. "All of this shit needs to be tested. You can't tell me your sick brother didn't bring Avery here. Or other vics. I'll bet my left nut that we'll find Avery's DNA…" He trails off. "Holy shit."

He's putting in a call before I can process what I'm seeing.

I stand frozen, every muscle corded tight, looking down at my brother's mutilated body. The word *corpse* hits me hard and fast, knocking the breath from my lungs.

His black suit is shredded, dried blood staining the expensive material from slashes across his chest. Throat sliced so deeply, his head is nearly severed from his body. As I take in the carnage, the only thought circling my mind is how he would hate to be seen like this. His face bruised. That perfect suit, ruined.

"Don't touch anything," Carson instructs. And it's like his order finally gives me permission to move.

I drop down and feel for a pulse. His skin is cold. Not ice-cold, the way you'd assume death would feel. But rather a chilly, air-conditioned temperature. As if he's become just another inanimate object in the room. His glassy blue eyes stare wide and vacant right into mine.

"I said, not to touch anything." Carson says something else into his phone, then steps beside me. "Mother fucker. Julian was just a slimy piece of business shit, after all. I guess this proves he's not the perp."

In two moves, I'm off the floor and have Carson jacked up by his shirt collar. I back him against the wall where my fist drives into his face. "This proves it?" I shout, sending another punch into his stomach. He tries to double over, but I keep him held upright. "All this time, you could've been investigating the real killer, but you had it in for my brother. Satisfied now?"

He sucks in a breath and manages to knock my arm away. He takes a swing and lands a strong right hook to my jaw. My vision explodes with white. His arms reach around my middle and he drives me backward.

My feet fail to push back against his momentum, and I fall, leaving a huffing Carson looking down at me. "Yeah. He's cleared. But what about you?" he grates. "There's still a matter of the evidence. Rope—just like yours— being used at a damn crime scene."

Pushing to my knees, I deliver a punch to his gut. Then land another to his face when he buckles. I look straight into his eyes as I get up and grab his neck. "You think I killed my own brother? You twisted fuck." I punch him in the stomach. "I was with Sadie last night. Then I was with your ass all day. What about you? What's your alibi?"

He coughs, wiping blood from his lip with the back of his hand. A slow smile curls his mouth. "If I was going to get rid of him, I wouldn't do it now. Not when I was so close to nailing him."

I shake my head, anger ripping through every muscle. My knuckles throb, my hand fisted so tight…just looking for the next place to stick Carson. Shoving him back, I say, "You're not worth it. Get out."

"Not happening. This is a closed crime scene now." He motions around the room. "Don't you think it's just a little too convenient that the owner of The Lair winds up dead? What about the missing footage from last night and this morning? Why would the UNSUB need to knock off Julian? What's your brother's part in all this?" His gaze sharpens on me. "Just because he's not the perp, doesn't mean he's not connected."

"His death could have nothing to do with this case at all." Given the number of enemies my brother's made over the years, that's not a complete stretch.

His eyes widen. "Really? I admit he doesn't fit the victimology. Unless he's hiding a vag beneath those slacks, he's not really the UNSUB's type. But he's linked to this, Colton. You know it. Give up what you're hiding."

As I turn my back to him, he clocks me hard across the back of my head. Blind fury rips loose, blocking the pain, and I unleash a growl as I tackle him to the floor. I wail on his face until a loud beeping breaks through the adrenaline haze.

I stumble off Carson and look around the room, recognizing the emergency signal. "Where is that coming from?"

Carson rolls to his side and spits blood into his hand. "Fucking hell. We just trampled and bled all over this crime scene." He winces as he pulls his phone from his coat pocket. "Quinn's going to fucking bench me for sure this time."

"What's coming from your phone?" My adrenaline is still pumping, my limbs quaking as the sudden concern for Sadie overtakes my need to pulverize Carson.

He shakes his head. "It's a video. I don't know—" He squints at the screen, his eye already starting to swell. "Shit. It's a video of Avery."

I get to my feet and stand behind Carson, my brother and this whole fucked-up room forgotten when I see the scene playing out on the screen. My stomach bottoms out.

Last night, Sadie whispered her secrets to me in the dark. In my arms, safe and sheltered, she told me about the physical dungeon that held her captive for days when she was young. About the man who stole her childhood. Who abducted and tortured her—the reason she fears chains, and touch…and herself.

She bared that secret in such descriptive detail, as if she was reliving every second. She trusted me so implicitly, that I listened—sick with fury—as she uncoiled every detail from her memory. I listened, unable *not* to see her words through my own eyes.

Now, looking at Carson's phone, it's as if I'm watching her memories play out. Hearing her pain all over again in surround sound as Avery's screams bleed from the speakers.

The woman on the screen—Avery—is dressed in a

pink tank top. Just like Sadie wore all those years ago. Her legs are naked and battered. Just the way Sadie was found. Even Avery's hair is the same shade as Sadie's dark tresses.

And the cane connecting with Avery's back...

I shut my eyes against the image.

It's nothing like what Sadie and I shared last night, as I endeavored to drive her demons away, giving her a piece of me and accepting her in turn. This is something evil. Vile. Pure and sinister. The abuse Avery's suffering in that video is just that. Abuse. And her captor is the only one receiving.

I hear Carson scramble to stand. "Jesus Christ. Is this being sent to everyone?"

And like that, my eyes fly open and I'm grabbing the device out of his hand.

The fight still hasn't left him, and he takes a wild swing, but I block his arm. "We're done!" I shout.

"That's fucking evidence! And it's mine," he says.

I know it's wrong...but I can't stomach the thought of Carson watching. I know what the UNSUB is recreating with this video. The scene he's methodically orchestrated to depict Sadie's torture. Having Carson witness something this personal to her...watching a moment in time when she was so vulnerable...

I squeeze the phone until I hear a *crack*.

Bringing myself back to my senses, I release the device. "Here," I say, shoving it against Carson's chest.

"Find out if everyone in the department saw that, or if it was just us."

But truthfully, I already know the answer. That scene was staged just for Sadie, whether or not the UNSUB meant for it to get to me, he wanted her to witness his act. I know she watched it. I can damn near feel her fear traveling right to me, this second. I whip out my phone and hit her number. Desperate, needing to hear her voice.

It goes to a generic voicemail recording.

"Fuck!"

Carson looks at me, then at my dead brother. "Shit, man. You're having a bad day."

It should sound as smug as his face—but I can actually hear empathy in his voice.

Scrubbing a hand through my hair, I look down at the floor. "Stay if you want, but I have somewhere to be."

Sadie's promise won't mean shit after this video.

But I'm keeping mine.

I take off down the stairs, hating myself for ever letting her out of my sight.

TRACE

SADIE

Everyone has a cherished object that transforms them. Changes them—even if just for a moment—into something else.

It could be a new pair of jeans. A fit so damn sexy it makes you put a little more swing in your hips. A cherry-red convertible so panty-dropping hot, it gives you a boost of confidence and the sex drive to match.

Whatever your poison, there's an object to get you there. It's a psychological phenomena that offers a perception of invincibility. Without it, we may never work up the courage to ask that certain someone out. Or demand that raise we know we deserve.

Those are all very obvious examples of lives that have never rocked on the edge—that have never been submerged in darkness. Devoured by its cruelty. But what about those of us who have? What do we deem necessary to transport us?

There's an object that I valued. One that I used to wear to transform myself. Or more accurately—reveal a hidden side. That person only surfaced when my demons raged, and I needed to unleash the monster within to quiet them.

When I lost that object, however, I thought it was a sign. Perhaps it was time to try a different way to sate my inner demons. Discover a new, safer path where I didn't have to loathe myself.

As I watch the tiny screen, hearing the shriek of absolute suffering, the scene playing out should mortify me. All that pain…all that anguish…should bombard me and make it impossible to discern any one signifying object in the dungeon.

But my eyes zero in on that small, revealing piece.

Hanging around Avery's neck, it's the only thing out of place in the scene. It doesn't belong. I didn't own the trinket when I was abducted at sixteen. It's what he wants me to see. I'm the only one who can recognize the flaw.

He hasn't wanted me all this time. No, he's been trying to bring *her* back. The woman who slipped that necklace on as if she was slipping into a second skin. Who caressed the crest of the Blood Countess as she prowled the edge of the night.

The monster I tried to bury.

"Sadie." Quinn's voice draws me out of my troubled

thoughts. I glance up from my phone as he steals it from my hands. "Watching it again won't help. You're just torturing yourself."

He's right, of course. Watching Avery suffer the same torture I endured all those years ago will do nothing to help her. But it does help me cope with what I have to do next.

"I know it's difficult," he continues. "But it's at least proof that she's still alive. We still have time to find her."

I push the heels of my hands into my eyes, as if I can scrub away the images seared into my retinas. "I know, Quinn. Trust me…I'm just tired of sitting idle."

A doctor appears from around the corner and Quinn stands to meet her. "Is she awake?"

The doctor purses her lips disapprovingly. "She is. But I have to insist that you make this quick, detective. Though her vocal chords weren't damaged to the extent we first thought, she's suffered severely and is under heavy pain medication. She needs rest to recover."

Quinn nods. "Thank you. We appreciate your help."

He hands me back my phone as the doctor leads us into Carmen's hospital room. A plastic breathing apparatus covers the lab tech's mouth, and a loud beeping emits from a machine beside her bed.

The doctor draws the curtain, giving us some privacy as the nurses continue to monitor her condition.

"Carmen," Quinn says, his notepad drawn and pen at the ready, just like the good detective he is. "I'm Detective

Quinn. This is Agent Bonds. We need your help to catch the person responsible for your attack. Are you able to do that?"

Weakly, her eyes blink open and she nods against the pillow.

"That's great. Do you recall what the offender looked like?"

She shakes her head.

He frowns. "That's okay. Was it because he knocked you unconscious? Do you remember the attack?"

She shakes her head again. Then slowly lifts her hand and points to her face. When Quinn only stares, she blinks a few times and waves her hand over her face.

"He wore a mask," I offer.

She nods.

"What about height? Build?" Quinn asks.

After a hard swallow that looks painful, she pushes the breathing apparatus aside and whispers, "Tall. Maybe just under six feet. Skinny."

Quinn jots down the note. "Hair color?"

"I don't know…maybe dark brown. Average. Short."

"That's good, Carmen. Thank you." With noticeable effort, Quinn prepares to ask her the tougher questions. The ones we're really here for. "Carmen, did he say anything to you?"

She blinks. Shakes her head.

I lay my hand on her arm, and she looks into my eyes. "Carmen. You're not in trouble for anything. Nothing you tell us will incriminate you. You're a victim. But Avery really needs your help. Anything you can tell us at all about your attacker or why you think he targeted you might save her life."

Her hand trembles as she pulls it away to wipe a tear streak from her cheek. She breathes slowly for a few seconds, then, "Avery found something on one of the ropes. I was the only one in the lab that night…with her. When I heard about what happened to her…I got scared. That's why I didn't come in today."

Quinn smiles down at her. "It's okay. Like Sadie said, you're not in trouble, and I know this has been terrifying, but you're safe now. We just need to know if Avery took a sample. Did she do anything that night—?"

"She did," Carmen cuts in. "Right before I left. She logged the discovery and then took a sample to send off." She closes her eyes. "She gave it to me to put in outgoing forensics." Her eyes open. "I don't think…" She breaks off. "I don't think, at least I don't know, if she noted that before…"

"It's okay," I say, giving her hand a comforting pulse. "You've given us a lot to go on."

She nods. "If I had any idea at all what would've happened, I never would've left—"

"You did the right thing, Carmen," Quinn says. "Avery gave you a directive and you followed it."

We leave Carmen as she begins to drift from the pain medication.

As we reach the parking lot, Quinn says, "Any chance we can intercept that sample before it reaches forensics?"

"Doubtful. But evidence stays on backlog there. Unless Avery put an urgent status on it to have the sample pushed ahead, then it's safe to assume it's just sitting there."

"But she knows how important that finding is," Quinn offers.

I shake my head, thinking. "But she also knows the profile. If she realized that the offender could be someone within the system, then she wouldn't call attention to it. That's why she didn't log sending out the sample. It has to be." I look at Quinn. "She wanted a backup."

He runs a hand down his face, looking agitated. "Then we can't call attention to it, either."

I'm putting a lot of faith in Avery—but she's never let me down before.

As I reach Quinn's car, I say, "Carmen doesn't strike me as the one who's been leaking to the press."

"No," he says, unlocking the Crown Vic with the keyless entry. "She comes across as a very frightened lab tech."

"Trust your gut," I say, repeating Avery's message to me. "My gut's telling me to have the sample tested in-house. Do we have any lab techs that we trust as much as Avery?"

Quinn stares up at the sky, shuts his eyes. Then he pulls his phone from his pocket. "Kyle, get in touch with Agent Proctor and have a team assembled and ready for a

UC operation. I'm on my way." A beat. "I don't care if Proctor will take issue. Get his ass there now." He cuts the call off.

"What are you planning?" I ask as he ducks into the car. I open my door and drop onto my seat. "Quinn? Talk to me. I need to know whatever is going through your head."

He cranks the engine. "Even if we recover the sample and test it ourselves, and even if the UNSUB's DNA is in the database, it's going to take hours to match."

"Not if we limit the scope of the search to people within the department."

"Still, we're taking a huge gamble on recovering the sample and matching it before the UNSUB knows what we're up to." He glances at me before he steers onto the main road. "We're only slightly ahead right now because there's a possibility that the UNSUB doesn't know about the sample."

I catch on. "But when we run it through CODIS, he will."

"But what if we draw him out and away from Avery first? Keep him preoccupied while we run the search. Just long enough to find a match and try to narrow down his location."

There's only one way to do that. "You want to use me as bait."

I see Quinn's face flush from my peripheral. "No. Absolutely not."

But he's already given himself away. I know when Quinn's trying to lie to me. "It's fine, Quinn. That was my initial tactic, if you recall."

He huffs out a long breath. "I'm not putting you in danger, Sadie. I promise you that. But we might actually be able to put the Feds to good use. They're already covering The Lair."

I shake my head. "The last sting you set up at the club went badly. The UNSUB won't fall for it." A sick feeling rocks my stomach. "And what if he's not in any database? We're taking more than a gamble…we'll be risking Avery's life if this fails."

Quinn takes a right into the station. "Then we won't fail. Whether or not that sample pans out, you said you could get inside the UNSUB's head." He sends me a serious look. "Avery's running out of time."

The pressure that's been mounting all day boils over.

Yes, I can get inside the UNSUB's head. I can think on his level. I've done it before…but I'm not sure if I can pull myself back out this time. It's a gamble on myself, too.

I swore to Colton that I wouldn't risk myself—that I wouldn't lose any part of me to the UNSUB. I have to keep that promise for more than his sake.

I flip my phone around and open the video. A still image of Avery shackled in chains displays on the screen. Her once shimmery blond hair is muted in tones of dull brown. Her eyes lifeless as she tries to separate herself from the weak woman being broken.

I know that struggle; I was successful at it. During my abduction, I achieved the ability to splinter my world. Becoming one girl who refused to be broken, who fought her captor to maintain her sanity...and another who crumbled, accepting her punishment.

My captor taught me so much; he was my mentor.

Remember your lessons...

His voice is the lurking demon in my mind.

Closing the video, I turn toward Quinn. "If we do this, it's my way. You want me to get inside his head and draw him out...fine. But don't question my methods. You or the Feds can't interfere."

"That won't be a problem." As Quinn parks, his hands stay gripped around the steering wheel, his gaze staring through the windshield. "Would this be happening if I'd listened to you two years ago about Connelly?"

A wave of guilt crashes over me. "We're all culpable, Quinn. I could've tried harder, presented more evidence... and you could've been a little less stubborn and pig-headed."

He lets a laugh slip. "Pig? Really? Going right for the cop jokes."

I shrug. "Even if we'd caught Connelly back then, there's no certainty that he would've given up his apprentice."

He looks at me then. "But there was a chance."

I hold his gaze. "There's still a chance."

His mouth parts, but then he presses his lips into a hard

line. He tries to voice his thoughts again as he averts his gaze from mine. "About Connelly…"

I grab the door handle. "Do you really want to go there now? There's no going back once we cross that line, Quinn. And we still have a lot to do before then."

He nods solemnly. "You're right," he says, meeting my eyes. "And even then, I'm not sure I want to know."

That truth resonates in the small span of space between us, thickening the air into a solid barrier.

I pull the handle and get out.

PREPARATION

COLTON

The green dot on my phone propels me on, my feet devouring the distance between me and Sadie. I head down a hallway of the ACPD building, taking a right up a flight of stairs to the third level.

"I broke protocol by not reporting Julian's murder to Quinn right away," Carson says from behind. "Don't think he's going to tolerate paranoia as an acceptable explanation."

"The UNSUB is able to hack into your department and send videos to your phones," I say, not slowing my pace. "It's not paranoia. It's taking the offensive."

"Still means an ass of paperwork for me."

My destination blinks on the screen, and I stand paused

at the door, my hand gripping the doorknob. "After the grief you gave my brother, I hardly think a little paperwork is punishment enough."

I turn the knob and step into the room. When my eyes find Sadie, the tension that's been gathering inside me since I first saw that video dissolves. My shoulders loosen a little more with each step closer to her.

Her gaze lifts from the table where her, Quinn, and a few other people stand around. She must see the anxiety still clinging to me because she doesn't say anything, just leaves the table to meet me in the middle of the room.

"What's wrong? Oh, my god. What happened to your face?" She touches the tender bruise along my jaw.

Pulling away from her touch is the last thing I want to do, but I'm eager to get her away from the others. "Let's leave here. Just for a little while."

Her eyebrows draw together. The urge to run my thumb down the crease thrums through me, wanting to smooth away all the worry from her face.

At her nod, I grasp her hand and lead her into the hallway, where I can't suppress my need any longer. I pull her into my arms. Bury my face in her hair. "I got in to it with Carson."

She releases a small laugh. "Well, from the looks of *his* face, you got the better of him."

My insides swell at hearing the relief in her voice, but it vanishes just as quickly. "Julian's dead," I say.

Her slight frame tenses in my arms, and I hold her tighter. "Colton…are you all right?"

I inhale her scent of lavender, her hair soft against my cheek. "I'm fine. It's not me I'm concerned about."

She pushes back. "He was your brother. You're in shock."

I glance around, not feeling alone enough in this hallway. "I can't talk about it here."

"All right. Come on."

I follow her to an outside corridor along the side of the building, inhaling deeply as the fall air blasts my face. "We shouldn't be here," I say, planting my back against the brick wall.

"Now that the FBI have intervened, I agree with you." Her green eyes squint against the sunlight, and I take her hand, bringing her closer. "What happened to Julian?"

I tamp down the burning ache in my chest. "I think he was the one who deleted the surveillance at the club. I can't prove it, and luckily neither can Carson, but Julian was involved. Knowing my brother, he was probably making money somehow off the sadistic fuck."

Sadie bites her lip, sending a pang of need right through me. "How was he killed?"

"I left before anyone examined him, but it looked close to the other murders. Close enough for Carson to implicate him." I expel a heavy breath, shaking my head. "But I'm not sure. Not really. For all I know, the UNSUB killed him to get back at me."

Sadie's mouth turns into a tight frown. "That's not a part of his methodology, Colton. If he did kill your brother, it's because he felt Julian was a loose end. I think he's been trying to eliminate those today."

I squint. "*If*? You think someone else could've killed my brother?"

"After today, after seeing and talking with a victim he supposedly left alive, I have my own reservations."

"So what, someone killed Julian and framed the UNSUB? I guess it wouldn't be the first time that's happened, right?"

"Colton. This is not your fault. None of this is on you—"

I stop her with a kiss. I've been dying to taste her lips since I first glimpsed her, safe and *here*. Not out chasing down a killer. As I pull away, I push a stray wisp of hair from her eyes. "I know, goddess. Believe me, I don't doubt for a second that my brother implicated himself somehow. I just need to figure out the *how* before Carson does."

She cranes an eyebrow. "Is that why you and Carson both showed up black and blue?"

I lock my arms around her back. "Part of it. I didn't want him to have the time to riffle through Julian's stuff."

"And your answer was to kick his ass?" A faint smile touches her lips. "Wish I could've seen it."

The smile forming on my mouth falls. "But you did see something," I say, carefully hinting to the video of Avery.

Her beautiful features contort. She looks away, facing

into the breeze whipping her hair over her shoulders. "I'm sure that was the UNSUB's last message to me. If we don't find him soon, Avery won't make it."

My thumb rubs the skin peeking between her jeans and shirt. "What's the message, Sadie?"

The small knot of her throat bobs. "Meet with him," she says. Then, looking at me, "And come alone."

A pang knocks my stomach. "And you think that's the only way to save Avery."

"It is," she says assuredly. "But it's not me he's asking…"

At my confused expression, she rests her head against my chest, her whole body one heartbeat of pain.

Linking my arms around her, I swallow hard before my next question. "Then who is he asking?"

She tilts her head back until her eyes meet mine. "The killer."

HER

UNSUB

She didn't scream.

That's what snared my attention. Drew me to the edge of the woods and held me captive. They always scream…

But not her.

I had my orders; my mentor had prepped me well. Grab the grungy little whore from the bar and leave before anyone noticed. She was to be his reward for doing away with the troublesome profiler.

But once I saw *her*, the vixen in red, I couldn't help myself. I needed more. After all, *he* was the one devolving, becoming unhinged. He was the one suffering the attention from her profile being passed around the department like the two-cent whore in my arms. Not me.

I was a nobody. I could disappear easily. And I would…but first, I needed to witness the destruction of such a beautiful creature.

Envy clutched me. I *was* envy.

He sent me on a rookie's errand to keep me busy while he had all the fun.

So I killed the bitch quickly.

I choked the life right out of her. No teasing out the pleasure, no enjoyment, and certainly no fulfillment. It was simply a task that had to be done in order to shut her up. Because I needed to watch.

My cock hadn't stirred once while I throttled the whore. It lay limp in my pants until I saw Connelly slice her dress and tear it from her body.

My dick twitched, becoming hard and demanding attention as I watched him stroke her chest. She had suffered abuse before—oh, how fucking divine. I saw that, too. During the trucker's little escapade in the bar. She doesn't like to be touched; downright fears it. And that gorgeous scar is the proof of her torture.

No wonder she won't gift Connelly her sweet screams.

She's been broken before.

As Connelly pushed her down onto the mud-sodden earth, I used the hooker beneath me to get some relief. My aching cock throbbed, and the whore was still warm. I lowered my zipper and pushed my erection against her bare thigh.

He won't be too disappointed in me. Look at his prize.

Just look at her! If she were mine, I could feast off her last moments for months. She'd quench this growing, insufferable thirst that's been tormenting me my whole life.

I had never wanted anything more than I wanted her in that instant.

Thinking back on it now, I did want her to end him.

I couldn't admit that until now. Maybe I even dragged out my desire for revenge a little longer than needed just for an excuse to seduce her. Truthfully, she intimidated me. I knew it the second she walked through those doors.

I would have to...*evolve* before I'd be anywhere near her match.

But let me finish my story...because, oh, it gets much better. Just remembering the good part has my hands fisting Avery's hair at the scalp, anticipating the ending.

Connelly, like the true amateur that he was, didn't respect her, didn't appreciate the extraordinary creature he'd lured into his woods. He straddled her like a common slut, his knife poised to take her life too quickly. He underestimated her; but I knew she would show him.

She never screamed.

She lifted her chin, exposing her creamy flesh, taunting him. And how she taunted. She knew his weakness; he would have to spend an extra moment worshiping her neck —it was his favorite.

And it worked. He stuck the knife into the ground above her head, then wrapped his hands around her neck, unable to deny himself the feel of her. My cock jumped, and I scrambled on top of the whore like a clumsy, horny adolescent to get a better view. I wanted to look into her eyes, just like he was.

I was beyond jealous. I *was* envy.

Then, right as I presumed she'd begin to lose consciousness, she moved beneath him, undulating her hips, thrashing, tempting him further. I was a throbbing puddle by this point…so completely paralyzed yet at the same time, tempted to slit Connelly's throat myself. Just to taste her sweet death in his place.

As soon as the thought entered my mind, she moved. So delicately, like the flutter of a Monarch's wings, she reached down and slipped off her heel. The spike drove into my mentor's neck. Blood rained down, covering my beauty in red, splattering her hair and luminescent skin.

He clutched the shoe as she pushed him aside like a maggot; not even a full-fledged predator to be feared. She stood above him, soaked in blood, her stained skin glistening in the moonlight.

I was riveted.

Of course, I had the choice to stop it. She was taking away my mentor, my master, the man who took me under his wing and improved me. But I couldn't stop watching. And, oh, how I loved to watch.

She transformed before my eyes, shedding her vibrant outer layer, a brilliant metamorphosis as she stripped of her cocoon and expanded her wings.

Those are the wings I craved.

I would forever long to be swept up into her guidance.

I knew, right then, that she wouldn't run for help. She wouldn't seek her phone, or radio in the attack. She didn't walk through those bar doors with that ending in mind. I spotted it right away—what Connelly had missed: she's a hunter.

While Connelly stalked her, she was drawing him into her web.

There was no victim in her.

I never touched myself through the whole scene. As my love looked down on her prey, fighting to staunch the bleeding, desperate to escape her claws, she swooped down and grabbed the knife.

She knelt in the mud—just as he had done to her—and whispered something into his ear. I craved so badly to know what it was. I would know. One day, I would find out.

And as she drew back, she let him see the blade coming for him. She moved purposely, methodically, savoring the fear in his eyes as she severed his carotid. One clean, perfect slice. No hesitation.

I came then. I came hard and furious, the release almost costing me my hiding place as I buried my mouth against the whore's breast to muffle my cry. I groaned into her dead flesh, my whole body alive and pulsing.

Pure rapture.

I was no longer envy; I was ecstasy.

Ecstasy, I had tasted it. Desire, I had felt it. Obsession…I *was* obsession.

Obsession would rule me until I was strong enough to own this marvelous creature.

I shut my eyes, allowing the memory to entice me, anticipation quaking through my hands. We're so close now. I uncurl my fingers from Avery's hair and stroke the necklace chain.

She goes rigid in my lap. I don't even have to say a word. After our last session, her fear for me is complete.

I twist the necklace until her skin puckers and I can feel her breaths through the vibration of the chain. The crest stands out against her soft flesh. I run my thumb over the white and red design, feeling bound to my love.

I plucked it from the muddy earth, wiped it clean. Cherished it as I delved into Sadie's world to unlock her secrets. And now, it's time to return it to its rightful place around her neck.

The moody trance is disturbed when a beep sounds from the corner.

I leave Avery in a curled pile on the blanket and pick up the phone.

Sadie: *I got your message. If you want the Countess, then you have to meet on my terms. You know where. I'll be there, waiting. Tonight.*

A vicious shiver races over my skin.

Tonight.

COVET

I t's impossible to measure the scope of any one person's struggle. Or to judge them based on yours.

This case has impacted everyone working it on a personal level.

I watched silently and passively, feeling helpless, as Colton made the dreaded phone call to his parents about his brother's death. According to him, he hadn't spoken to them since before he fled his hometown. Now, his first communication with them in so many years is to deliver news that will forever leave them questioning *why*?

And though he may try to disguise the anguish he feels at having lost his brother, I know that it's affecting him deeply. They never resolved their issues, never made their peace over the love they shared for one woman. Colton will bear that guilt in the way Colton handles everything: he'll consume the pain, make it a part of himself. And I'll be there—in the shadow of our world—to bear it with him.

Quinn is the toughest to uncover, with his thick skin and hard-boiled detective attitude. He comes across as unmovable as a steel beam, and just as dense. But even he's been pushed beyond his breaking point, the fight inside him surfacing and cracking his tough exterior.

He's a creaking branch bowing beneath the pressure of this case. Just as everyone is being changed, he won't come out unscathed. He'll have his own brand of scars, and he'll use them to continue to fight the evil of this world. That's who he is.

I look around from my safe and secluded spot in the conference room, regarding each member of the task force with the same discretion. There is no clear certainty to tonight's ending. Every single member of this department will be tested and challenged.

Even Carson, with his superior demeanor will fall victim to the unknown. I think he will suffer that more than most; he doesn't do well with what he doesn't understand. It's best if he remains in that dark, for his own survival.

As Quinn gives the final instructions to his task force, Agent Proctor readies his troop of Feds. The combined efforts of both our numbers covering The Lair will ensure the UNSUB doesn't move unnoticed tonight.

"The Feds are all about staking out the club," Quinn

says, pulling up a chair beside mine. "Told you we could use them. And Proctor located that girl. Turns out, she's not just a member, she's a pro."

I raise my eyebrows. "The UNSUB recruited a sex worker to wear a red wig and dress like me. Not sure how I feel about that." My tone is rimmed with humor, but that's only to disguise the disturbed feeling wiggling inside me. The very definition of irony is a pro pretending to be me, when I once played her part. A coincidence or convenience? Everything the UNSUB does is calculated.

When Colton was lured outside the club a few nights ago by a woman who he thought was me, then jumped by the unis staking out the club, at the time, I didn't see the connection. I assumed Carson had set the trap. But when Colton mentioned her again, sitting at the table where I frequent, I decided it was time to find my doppelganger and put her to good use.

"She confirmed a man from the club paid her. Even gave her the dress and wig to wear," Quinn says.

"No chance there's trace on the dress," I say, knowing the UNSUB made sure to leave no evidence of himself.

He sits back. "It would be just too easy if Locard's principle applied to this case, wouldn't it?"

I smile. "The exchange principle," I say. "Every perp leaves something behind and takes something with him. You continue to surprise me, Quinn."

He lets my compliment slide. "The dress is with the techs at the lab. But I'm more interested in her description of him." Quinn presses his fingers to his brow, apparently working out a headache. "It matches Carmen's description perfectly. The damn UNSUB has been there, this whole time, right in the open, and we never saw him. It feels like he's not even trying to hide…and we've been letting him get away with it."

I go to lay my hand on top of Quinn's, then decide against it, and instead reach for my phone. "We're not letting him get away with anything." I tap my screen, opening the messages I've exchanged with the UNSUB.

We're just a couple short hours away from initiating the UC operation, and I'm uncharacteristically calm. I've done this before, but never involving anyone else. I keep looking for a sign from the UNSUB that he's backing out —but he's been anticipating this moment for two years. He won't disappoint me.

"Sadie?"

I look up. Colton is there, amid the commotion and preparation for the operation, my focal point to keep me grounded.

I turn to Quinn. "I'm going to get ready."

He nods, and for a brief moment, it looks like he's about to say something. But just as I won't offer him comfort with a touch, he won't unmask his feelings with words.

There's still too many unresolved things between us before that can happen.

He looks away from me. "Make sure you check in for your final briefing before you set out."

I smile inwardly. "I will."

The hollow *click* of my key turning the lock echoes throughout my apartment. I stand here, immobile, feeling the press of Colton's intense presence against my back. He rests his hand over mine, his strong chest a solid embrace of comfort as he wraps an arm around my waist.

"You don't have to do this," he says, nuzzling into my neck.

I inhale his masculine scent; a mix of the club and something indefinably Colton. Sandalwood and cologne, and all male. It bolsters my resolve, and I turn the knob.

My apartment feels void and unlived in. The only time I've spent here recently was to rush in and out. The mood of high anxiety still lurks in the chilly air.

I set my keys and bag on the living room table, my gaze trailing Colton as he moves around the room. "Nothing's changed for me. You can't scare me away," he says, his fingers roaming over my fireplace mantel. There are no pictures there. Just my obscenely embarrassing porcelain figurine collection.

"Not even with my creepy porcelain dolls?" I ask, trying to affect a light tone and failing miserably.

Colton gifts me with a faint smile anyway. "You like them because they're fragile. Breakable. Beautiful. You like to protect them."

I head toward my bedroom, saying as I pass, "I'm that transparent, huh?"

He reaches out and grabs my hand, pulling me to a stop. "Only to me."

Licking my lips, I stare into his pale blues. "That night in the club…I told you. I'm a monster. It's the truth of me. I've never admitted that to anyone, Colton. What I shared with you today is who I am. Unlike you, I have never felt any mercy."

Taking my hands in his, he laces our fingers together. "But you're wrong, goddess. You felt mercy for the victims."

I shake my head. "I felt retribution. It's not the same."

"We *are* the same." His eyes bore into me, down to my marrow. "If you claim otherwise, then everything you demanded I believe last night is a lie. And I won't let it be. Even if I was so desperate for your acceptance that I didn't question *why* or *how* you could love a villain."

"I meant it all. But now you see who the real villain is," I say, my voice low, my soul fractured and just as desperate to hear Colton's affirmation of me.

"If that's so, then is it the only reason you're with me? Because you believe your sin is greater than mine?"

The leaden truth of that question crushes me. "No... You know it's more than that."

"We're bound together," he says, bringing my body flush against his. "Whether that's in sin or mercy, I don't care to make the distinction. It's just one more reason, one more undeniable proof, that you were designed for me."

His lips find mine then. Tasting of solace and benevolence and unyielding consequence. Temptation to be lost—just leave behind all my pain and suffering, and the woman who clung so ruthlessly to it—bewitches me. I could truly let go.

I would never look back.

But a *beep* from my phone pulls me out of that fantasy. Breaking away from Colton's firm embrace, I glimpse the screen, and I'm plunged right back into the icy waters of reality. As if I were ever able to escape.

An image of Avery wearing a tight, silky red dress flashes across the screen, followed by a text: *A simple request, my love. See you soon.*

I swallow the thick bile coating my throat walls. "He wants me to wear a red dress."

Colton takes the phone, closes the message, and sets it atop the mantel. Anchoring his hands around my waist, he lifts me up until I'm forced to straddle his hips, my arms finding their home securely around his neck.

"If that's his request," he says, walking us into my bedroom, "then I have one of my own." He kisses the

155

column of my neck tenderly before he lays me down on the bed.

I rest my cheek against the cool comforter as I watch him open my closet door. "My dresses are all the way in the back," I say, trying to force away the thoughts of what Avery must be suffering this minute. *What is he doing to her in that dress?*

Avery is beautiful and pure—and she *was* perfect. My world has become darker and darker since my abduction, and I hate that someone so full of light has now been tainted by that same evil. Despite what I tried to turn away from, every molecule in my body wants to kill the evil that has corrupted her world and turned it into mine.

Colton steps out of my closet with a satin red dress. It's not exactly like the one I wore the night I stalked Connelly to that bar, but it's a close enough match.

I clear my throat. "I should've seen it before now. His ritual to decorate his victims in dresses. How could I have missed the connection?" I close my eyes. "My profiling skills should really be called into question."

The mattress dips under Colton's weight. "I *would* argue that…if you hadn't accused me of being a serial killer right off the rip."

I attempt to stifle it, but a laugh escapes. "We're completely twisted. The only two people who could find humor in any of this," I say, linking my fingers around his.

He brings my hand up and places a soft kiss beside the band of rope. "Stop questioning us, goddess. And stop doubting yourself. As selfish as this may sound, I don't regret anything that brought you into my world."

I reach over and palm his face, loving the feel of his unshaven scruff. "What's your request?" I ask, unable to restrain the rising desire unfurling within me. Before I go, before I risk everything...I need to feel Colton inside me once more. To know that I had finally found redemption.

Pressing into my palm, he turns his face to the side and catches my finger between his teeth. His tongue traces the tip before he releases me, sending a surge of yearning all the way down to my toes.

He pushes off the bed, stands at the base. Kneeling down to remove my shoes, he says, "The UNSUB wants *one* side of you; but I want it all. Who you were before, between, and now. You might have to dress the part for him...but I won't let you slide on that dress with him in your mind. You're mine, goddess. When you walk out that door, I want you to feel me—to know that I've touched and branded every part of you and that fucking dress."

He leans over me, one hand supporting his weight on the bed, the other skillfully unbuttoning my jeans. My stomach dips with a flutter as he slips his hand beneath the band and pulls them down my thighs.

I arch my back as he tugs my jeans all the way off, discarding them to the floor, his intense gaze never leaving mine. The cool kiss of air slides over my skin, making me shiver, as he grasps the hem of my shirt and pushes it toward my head.

He pauses just as the material covers my eyes, and his hands anchor my wrists to the bed. "I am so very tempted to take you right now." His whispered words graze my lips, then his mouth is on the swell of my breast, his tongue circling and tasting me.

A fierce ache blooms between my thighs. I lift my hips, making satisfying contact with the coarse jeans concealing his hardness. "Now," I beg.

I feel his smile against my skin. "Not yet."

The shirt clears my head, and Colton wastes little time removing the last articles of my clothing. The bra finds its place on the floor next to my underwear. I lay bare before him, the only item on my person the rope bracelet that claims me as his.

Only now, I can honestly say that every inch of my flesh belongs to him. And I bask in the knowledge that the man before me is mine. My gaze drags over his well-defined chest and chiseled stomach as he reaches behind his head and yanks off his shirt.

That one move slays me. I've seen him perform Shibari—his muscles gathering and flexing as he masterfully manipulates the rope, his body perfectly tuned to deliver pleasure. But here, right now, as he unbuckles his belt and pulls it through the loops, I swear, I've never seen him exude so much sex appeal.

He loops the belt in his hand, and I press my thighs together in anticipation. His lips twist into a sultry, crooked smile. "This isn't for you, goddess." He tosses the belt to the floor. "At least, not tonight." His pants drop, revealing his hard want as it strains against his black boxers.

He wraps his hand around his hard shaft and grips, sending a pleasurable quiver through me. "Stand up."

It's the first time I've been completely unbound with Colton—and yet, I've never felt more dominated. His deep voice wraps around me and commands my body to respond as if I'm tethered securely within his ropes.

"Place everything you're wearing on the bed," he says.

I move to my dresser, open the top drawer, and riffle through my lingerie. And understanding dawns: I'm no longer struggling to look the part for the UNSUB—I'm selecting items for Colton. This is for him.

I lay my choices atop the comforter, earning an approving grin from Colton. He takes his time, trailing his rough palms up my arms, across my back, along my hips. Touching every inch of me with sure, branding intent.

When he reaches my inner thigh, I close my eyes, knowing he'll feel how wet I am. He grazes my lips, thrumming my body, the aftershock of his touch making me quake. Then, with a guttural command, he flattens his hand against my back and pushes me chest-down on the foot of the bed.

His mouth finds my hot center in the next beat, and I gasp in a sharp breath at the feel of his tongue tasting me. Gripping my thighs, he spreads my legs wide, giving him unfettered access. My belly tightens as he slips a finger inside me, sampling, teasing, making me crave more.

An impossible task, but he manages to slide one of my stockings onto my toes, then up my calf. The whole while, his talented tongue and mouth never leave me. The feel of his hands working and caressing the silken material onto my body has me trembling for release. He stops when the stocking reaches my thigh.

"Turn around," he directs.

On shaky legs, I push myself up to stand and face him. Kneeling before me, he holds the other stocking. This slow perusal of my body is a new kind of torture. I'm tempted to straddle him—bring him to the brink with me.

But before that thought can be realized, he palms my calf and guides my toes into the stocking. He slowly drags it up my leg and, when he reaches my thigh, angles my leg over his shoulder. He grabs my ass, forcing my hips forward.

I tense as he sucks me into his mouth, his tongue firm and purposeful as it flicks over my clit. My hands go to his hair, gripping, needing support as I balance between ecstasy and falling. But my leg doesn't give out. I press into him, demanding. My body ordering him not to stop.

Only right when I feel the wetness slick my thighs, he pulls back. A moan of discontent slips free, and he groans. "Hand me the garter belt." I can hear the strain in his voice, the constraint.

It puts a wicked smile on my face to know he's near

breaking, too. I reach behind, grab the garter, dangle it above him. His eyes blaze with want as he tugs it from my grasp.

"You sure dressing me is what you really want to do?"

A smile slants his mouth. "Right this second...I really want to taste that sassy mouth." He rises onto his feet and cups my face, his lips crash against mine.

I reel back from the impact, desperate to find my footing and push all of my desire back against him...but just as quickly, he steps away, leaving me breathless and needy.

He stretches out the garter, testing its elasticity. "This could be put to better use," he says, slipping the black material around my waist. "But we'll save that for another night, too." As he connects the clasps, he works the belt down around my hips, his fingers dragging possessively over my skin.

Dropping to his knees, he cups my hips and nips the tender flesh of my belly. I flinch, and he continues to kiss and bite his way toward my mound. Taking his time there, he runs a strap of the belt through his fingers—the same way I've seen him toy with his ropes—then tugs it down where he attaches it to the stocking.

With just as much finesse and tenderness, he clasps the other ends of the garter belt to my stockings, his eyes intense, his purpose to claim me pouring through him with every exchange.

My eyes are closed, my whole body one heartbeat,

trusting him and anticipating his next move. I feel the heat of his skin against my nipples. They pebble, just as desperate for his attention. He never denies me.

He eases my arms into the straps of my bra, slowly, delicately, bringing them up to rest along my shoulders. The cups hang open at the swell of my breasts where he cups me and lowers his mouth to one nipple.

I tilt my head and arch my back, pressing as close to him as he'll allow. And as he transitions from one breast to the other, sending an erotic tingling right to my core, I squeeze my thighs together, capturing him there.

His teeth bear down on me, scraping my nipple as he rocks his hips, thrusting his hard cock between my clenched thighs. "I'm going to bury myself in you, goddess…"

His whispered promise against my skin heightens my arousal, and my hands cling to his back, my nails seeking purchase to sustain me.

Before he gives in to his desire to do just that, he forcefully breaks away. His clear blue eyes are ablaze with his every intent, unleashing a thrill within me. He draws the clasps of my bra together. My breasts feel heavy and achy, trapped and unsatisfied. But he continues to fondle them through the bra. He bites deeply, sinking his teeth into the padding, spiking my desire.

Backing up a step, he swings his gaze to the dress laid out on the bed. I'm so far from being ready—I'm damn near angry that I have to put it on.

As if reading my thoughts, he says, "The night you wore a red dress for me, and I had you on my bench...I had to forcefully restrain myself from taking you." His hands curl into fists. "I wanted to tear your clothes from your body. That's what you do to me, goddess. Make me into some kind of animal. But knowing you're going out there...to meet him? I'm feral. Marking my territory. Covering you in my scent." He draws closer, his body a fire-hot torch of lust. Then he reaches toward the bed and snags the dress.

Without request, I lift my arms above my head. His arms circle me, and I can feel the muscles of his arms flexing along my waist as he bunches the dress before he raises his arms alongside mine.

The satin material glides down my arms, whisper-soft, then travels over my body. Gently towing the hem down, Colton drags the dress toward my thighs. The material embraces my skin in a perfect fit as it molds to my curves.

He pushes my wrists behind my back, where he links them together with his hands. Trailing his lips over my neck, delivering soft kisses, he whispers, "So. Fucking. Beautiful."

A short time ago, that one word could decimate me—but Colton has given me ownership over it. I never want him to stop saying it—to stop seeing me as his beautiful goddess. I wriggle a hand free and find the band of his boxers. He doesn't stop me—wants me just as badly in this moment.

I push his boxers down and feel the spring of his erection against my stomach. Hard, needy, *mine*. Only he doesn't allow me the same indulgence. He has me in his arms and lifted against his chest before I can taste him.

My back meets the wall, and it's as if he needs to devour me whole—his hands seek my center, his fingers pushing inside me, readying me to take him—as his mouth and body pin me.

"Fuck me, Colton," I get out around his demanding kisses. "I need you hard and raw…inside me."

His growl rumbles against my chest as he positions his cock, his slick fingers rubbing me all over him before he thrusts up and drives into me. I wrap my legs around him as he braces my arm against the wall. He slams into me again so fierce, my spine protests; but my body accepts the pain, requires it. I dig my heels into his backside, challenging more.

I'm untethered, but so completely bound to him. With every thrust, I climb. With every whisper of love and profession of lust, I know I can never be contented by this man—I will always *need*. But just as surely as he makes me insatiable, he fulfills me—utterly.

The overflow of emotion is almost painful. I am not a hollow vessel. I am not unfeeling or broken—I feel to the depth of my soul. The darkest part of me is alive—it stirs with an abundance of sensation and love.

And that emotion wraps around us now as Colton pushes off the wall and cradles me in his strong arms.

Gripping my shoulders, he plunges into me, deep and claiming. He stays there, filling me, demanding I take all of him. As he carries me to the bed, he lies back, offering me his control.

I'm empowered by the look in his eyes—the one daring me to accept every part of him in return. Linking my fingers through his, I rock my hips, loving the way his teeth sink into his lip at the feel of me tightening around him.

"Finish me, goddess," he says, his voice a low rasp.

It drives my desire to the brink—and I speed my movements, taking him deeper, almost unable to bear it the harder he becomes. But we were designed for each other— my channel slicking against him and welcoming his sizable length.

He releases my hand to clamp it around my nape, drawing me to him as he pushes up. His lips find mine, caressing hard. Passionate. His grip tightens as I moan against him, my back arching, forcing him to curve his hips as he drives into me with fierce need.

As my orgasm grabs hold, I raise up. His hands go to my thighs, gripping and guiding, as I let my head fall back. Completely lost to him. Our rhythm intensifies, and we meet each other with heavy, powerful thrusts that send me right over the edge.

He curses, and the guttural sound of his voice fires off a pulsing deep within my core. It surges into my stomach, my back. Through my whole body. A flowing current. My hips work harder, rocking and slamming against him as he thrusts to meet me each time. His fingers dig into my skin as his hands anchor to my hips.

And as I ride the electric currents, my hips undulating and swirling, his hip digs into my thighs as he arches and begins to pulse deep inside me. I fall against his chest, mine rising and falling in quick succession with his.

His fingers slide into my hair as he presses a tender kiss to the top of my head.

Inhaling his scent, allowing it to comfort me, keeping the night ahead at bay just a moment longer, I say, "We're going to need a second dress."

The rattle of his laugh tickles my chest. "Another round?"

I lift up, capturing his lips in an intimate kiss. Then I smile. "I'm game."

FINAL ACT

SADIE

An unmarked van is stationed two blocks from The Lair. Within, there's an assembled team with eyes and ears inside the club. Special Agent Proctor has Feds on the inside as well as the outside, and Quinn has the techs linked up to the club surveillance, sending a feed right to the monitors inside the van.

It's a perfect sting operation—that is, if it weren't for the fact that it's completely bogus.

"Are you sure the UNSUB won't show here?" Quinn asks as he clips a wire to the inside of my dress collar.

I tried to convince him that the wire was unnecessary —that the UNSUB will make sure I discard any monitoring equipment before he approaches me, but Quinn was adamant. I wasn't leaving his sight until I was bugged. I might've been wrong when I thought Carson would suffer the most; Quinn has never been able to accept anything less than orderly. And this scheme is anything but organized.

"This place is crawling with FBI," I say, noting an agent trying and failing to pass himself off as a member of a BDSM club. Dressed in all vinyl, he sports a chain belt with handcuff buckle. If my insides weren't numb with adrenaline, I might laugh. "One sure-fire way to keep a suspect away? Send in the FBI. If I can spot them, the UNSUB already knows they're here. Besides, you did a good job of leaking the operation around the department. He knows where the set-up is happening."

Quinn lowers his hands from my dress with an audible exhale. "Tell me again how you know this will work?"

"I relayed a message to him in my text. Something only he would understand and the Feds wouldn't. Trust me, Quinn," I say, locking gazes. "This will work. It has to." *Because Avery is out of time.*

Agent Proctor didn't question what *"You know where"* referred to in my text to the UNSUB. Since The Lair is the only common denominator linking most of the victims together, I let the assumption slide.

"I just can't believe Proctor thinks this obvious stakeout will get past anyone." I right my dress collar, and look up when Quinn doesn't respond. "What is it?"

His mouth creases into a tight frown. "My gut doesn't

like it. I think you should go ahead with the botched operation—"

"And leave Avery to suffer longer? Or worse…die? Avery needs this to happen, Quinn." Despite my own hesitations, I grab his hand, sending a sure pulse to his palm. I stay latched onto him until his hazel eyes warm. "Just keep Proctor and his team focused on The Lair, giving the techs enough time to run the DNA through the database. Trust the plan. Trust *me*."

Even though I mean every word, know that I don't have a choice but to succeed—I can't let Quinn see the fear harboring just below my surface. My plan only gets me face-to-face with the UNSUB. What then? Despite my past, regardless of what I've done, I don't know how this will end.

With a deep breath, Quinn nods. "Get your ass in there before lover boy starts to freak out."

I can't help it, I smile. Only the small relief doesn't last nearly long enough. Quinn's grip on my hand loosens, and before I can say anything, he walks away. I wait for him to send me a signal that once this is over, we'll be okay. But he doesn't look back, and I feel the loss of his protection.

I'm truly on my own.

From my spot on the corner of the building, I watch the pro—my doppelganger—be escorted into the van. Besides Carmen, she's the only person who's *possibly* seen the UNSUB and can make an identification.

Making sure Proctor and the team see me go into the

club, I walk straight through the front doors. If I didn't already feel like a spotlight was beaming right on me, as soon as I enter onto the main level, it's as if I'm walking onto a stage.

I slink past dancing bodies on my way to the bar. I get a curious glare from Agent Rollins at the other end, but I nod to the bartender, ignoring his assessment. She sets the shot of bourbon in front of me and I throw it back with force.

One for the nerves before I commit to this.

Letting the burn of alcohol warm my insides, I push away from the bar top and weave my way toward the spiral staircase. The beat of house music reverberates through my chest, pushing my feet faster up every step.

One of the bouncers nods for me to pass. I reach the office door, and Colton has it open before I knock.

"I saw you coming," he says as he rests his hand at the small of my back and leads me in. "Let's make this quick."

A petite UC agent stands beside Carson in the middle of the office. She greets me with a nod and an easy smile that feels at odds with this meeting. But I move hurriedly, unzipping the side of my dress and pushing it down my body.

Colton clears his throat. I look up to see him send Carson a stern glare. With an exasperated sigh, Carson turns to face the wall of monitors. "Nothing I haven't seen before," he says.

"Not from her, you haven't." Colton takes the dress as I hand it off to him, swapping it out for the satin one he dressed me in at my apartment. Even now, as he helps me slide it over my head, I feel his hands and mouth claiming my body.

The UC agent slips into my dress, allowing Carson to help her zip into it. From the back, she can pass as me. Her makeup and hair are a match, and in the dim lighting of the club, with agents that have only seen me during short periods, she can pull this off.

I step toward her and push the wire Quinn taped to my dress under the collar. "Be careful," I tell her.

"You, too," she says. "We're going to get this bastard, Agent Bonds."

I hold her green gaze, relaying a silent thanks. "We are."

"I need your phone," Carson says.

One less thing to be tracked with. I remove it from my clutch and hand it to him. "Don't let her out of your sight."

Our eyes meet, and understanding passes between us.

"Anything to get one over on the Feds. I'm onboard." A smirk lights his face.

Although Carson has been chasing the wrong man, he's been devoted to capturing a serial killer who's eluded him for two years. Even if I still don't trust him, I trust that he's committed to this operation. It's his chance to not only make amends, but to get retribution for his career.

I turn toward Colton. "I'm ready."

His hand is in mine, then he's leading me toward the other end of the office. "Only me and Julian know"—he cuts short—"Julian *knew* about this access."

He pushes aside a tapestry and reveals a door. "My brother made a lot of enemies," he says. "He always made sure to have a way to escape."

A pang hits my chest as I stare into his eyes, both of us leaving the truth unsaid. His brother didn't escape his fate, which may remain a mystery to Colton.

The dark hallway leads down a flight of stairs and to a back door, where Colton pauses. "I want you to take this." He holds out his phone—the one issued to him by the department.

"I can't," I say, shaking my head. "I can't have anything—"

"I disabled the GPS," he interrupts. "I hated doing it… because it's killing me to let you go out there with no way to find you. You're asking a lot of me, goddess. Almost too much. I have to at least know you have a way to call for help. If you need it."

I swallow, allowing Colton to wrap my fingers around the cool device. "I promise," I say, moving close to him. "I'm coming back to you."

He cups my face, kisses me with everything he has. I can feel his torment in that kiss—his absolute devotion and warring anguish.

As I pull away, he whispers, "I love you, goddess."

I know there's more to be said, so much more than that word can convey. But right now, it has to be enough. "I love you, Colton Reed." I release the strain from my lungs. "Make sure you show our girl a good time." I smile up at him.

"The crew is doing a special tribute to Julian tonight," he says. "I won't let her out of my sight. That, I promise." He pushes the door open. And even in the dim lighting of the street, I can see the tremor of his hand gripped tightly to the door. "I'll storm heaven and hell if you don't come back to me."

As I step onto the sidewalk, I say, "Hell's not ready for me yet."

In the distance, the lights of the Theodore Roosevelt Bridge flicker, peeking in and out of the trees like a movie reel flipping through a projector. The highway is teeming with cars, city-goers passing on their way into downtown.

I lean forward and knock on the plastic window between the cabdriver and me. "Pull over onto the median at the entrance to TRI, please."

He does as requested, and the cab comes to a stop on

the small strip of road. I push a few bills through the slot before my heels meet the uneven pavement. I twist my ankle and curse, righting myself as I make my way over first the gravel, then the grassy divider toward the extensive walking bridge connecting the mainland to the island.

The rancid smell of marshy river mixing with gas fumes drifting off the highway turns my stomach, reminding me of the morning the exsanguinated victim was discovered.

I pass the memorial with the TR statue, crossing onto the cemented bridge where a few ground accent lights illuminate the man-made pond and center fountain. Otherwise, it's near black out, with only the lights from the city and DC glowing against the skyline.

The UNSUB marked this island, giving me a targeted, unsubtle hint when he painted the reeds with his victim's blood. I didn't understand at the time why he chose to stray from his MO and chance being caught in broad daylight, in a place that's usually bustling with tourists.

But it's all very clear now.

On the other side of the island, just off the swamp trails, is where he bled the vic. In theory, that's where I should go—where the crime scene tape still marks off the blood-coated reeds, and the Bathory crest has been washed away by the rain, but still signifies his X marks the spot mentality.

But one: I'm wearing a dress and heels. Hiking into the

woods, and down through swampy marsh, then through river grass isn't happening. Two: he wouldn't have requested I wear something so unsuitable for the scene if he didn't plan to meet me in a more civilized setting.

And three: no damn way am I going off the beaten trail to meet a killer on his turf.

He's followed me here; he's watching me now. He can meet me halfway on this.

A snap draws my attention to the wooded surroundings of the memorial. I set my clutch down, silently removing my gun from the bag before I creep toward the darkness.

"We're alone," I call out. I hook my finger around the trigger. "I left them all back at the club."

Silence mocks me. Even the creatures stop stirring.

"Please don't shoot me," someone says.

"Hands up!" I shout. "Move into the light. Now."

"Jesus!" A guy dressed in a jean jacket and ball cap walks onto the memorial with his hands over his head. He holds a small paper-brown package in one. "I was just supposed to drop this off... Oh, my god. Is it drugs? Is this a trap?"

I keep my SIG aimed on him as I approach. "Drop the package." He does, and I pat down his front pockets. "Take out your ID...slowly!"

With trembling hands, the young guy—who looks no older than twenty—removes his wallet and hands it to me. "Are you a prostitute or something? Am I being robbed?"

"Stop talking," I snap. I look through his wallet, find

his driver's license and read off his name. "Mike Linsinski, who told you to bring this here?" I nod toward the package at his feet.

He rapidly shakes his head. "Some dude, ma'am. I don't know. He gave me some cash and said to bring it here. Fuck." He seals his eyes closed. "I'm an idiot."

"Yeah, you are." I bend down to pick up the package, a nervous flutter attacking my stomach. "Don't move, you hear me?"

At his adamant nod, I holster my gun under my arm and rip the package open. Inside, with dried blood staining the paper, my necklace rests on a bed of cotton.

My heart leaps into my throat. "Where's the man who gave this to you?"

He shakes his head again, arms still raised. "I was just walking around downtown. He approached me. I don't know the dude!"

Shit. *Shit, shit shit*! I run over to my clutch and pull out a pair of zip ties. Then I wrestle the guy's hands behind his back. "You're going to stay here. Do you get that? If not, I will hunt you down, Mike Linsinski. I know where you live."

He swears under his breath as I link his wrists together.

I stuff my gun and the necklace, with what I assume is Avery's blood, into my bag and kick off my heels. My feet slap the pavement as I race toward the bridge, but a cry slams me to a stop.

I glance back at the guy, but he's searching for the noise, too.

Another ear-splitting shout, and I'm pulling my gun; I know that voice—though I've never heard it in such anguish, I can still discern who it's from.

"Quinn!"

TIES

COLTON

The news of my brother's grisly death traveled through the scene like wildfire. With my personal cell phone confiscated by the cops, I've been out of touch, which raised an alarm for the club. And with the Feds infiltrating the scene, it seemed like a good time to shut the club down.

That is, until I returned this evening to find the club crew already organizing a tribute to Julian. Lilly Anne and Onyx did the work, contacting members and insisting I relax. *Relax*. That's not happening tonight.

Besides being in a constant state of worry over Sadie, the guilt has begun to eat at me. My main reason for agreeing to the tribute was because it would bring in a swarm of people, giving the UC agent enough cover to make Sadie's crazy plan work.

I've been able to dodge most of my brother's "investors." Those who still owe him money and who are anxious to be taken off his blackmail list. I've found my little, sacred corner of the voyeur room where I down a shot of bourbon, no one questioning my request to be left alone.

Even though my brother was trying to pull away from the scene, and despite the fact that he was never really in it other than to make money, I can't help but feel he would've been honored.

The stage is set for the scene to begin. Lilly Ann has stage-managed my brother's favorites: ménage à trois, girl-on-girl, and submission. He was never big into kink; liked to keep it simple. Which only reminds me that I somehow have to organize his funeral with his fiancé.

I tip back another shot.

Across from me, Carson sips on a non-alcoholic beer, keeping his head clear but trying to appear inconspicuous. Dressed down in jeans and a T-shirt, he still looks completely uptight and out of place.

Up ahead, a few tables closer to the stage, the UC agent watches the first scene. I admit, for the short briefing she had, she's doing a decent job at playing Sadie. She keeps to herself, fending off any advances, and doesn't invite any attention. But with the number of people here tonight, she wouldn't stand out. That's the idea.

I'm trying my best to be here, in the moment, and to pay Julian my respects despite every fiber of my being screaming to be with Sadie. Trust is not the issue—I trust her. I trust her to keep herself safe; she's handled herself in similar situations, and I have no care for the sick shit she plans to end tonight. I just can't stand the helpless feeling stealing over me, taunting me. Shouting that she's up against something deadlier and more dangerous than anything she's faced in her past.

Dammit it to hell. There's a sick roiling in the pit of my stomach tempting me to go after her.

I should've followed her.

"Relax," Carson says, his gaze steady on the stage. "She's not out there alone."

I glare across the table at him. "What are you talking about?"

He glances at me. "Did you really think Quinn would let her go off by herself to meet up with a fucking serial killer?" He chuckles. "Sadie's good, but she's no field agent."

Anger rips through my veins. "Who's out there with her?" I kick the leg of his chair, forcing his full attention on me. "Who the *fuck* is out there?"

It finally registers in his thick skull. His eyebrows pull together as he says, "I wasn't in on the side op. I was working the club angle with you and Sadie. Quinn put together—"

"Fuck." I leap up, rocking the table and knocking over

Carson's beer, and am weaving through the crowd before he can finish.

I've never trusted Quinn. Despite Sadie's reassurance —her own faith in the man—I've always been suspicious of his intentions where she was concerned. But motherfucker, I know he has feelings for her—so why the hell would he jeopardize her safety?

The UNSUB gets one whiff that Sadie set him up, and he'll...

I stop that thought. Right there in its tracks.

I hit the hallway where I'm shoved against the wall. Carson braces his forearm against my neck. "Whatever you're thinking about doing, *don't*." His eyes widen. "This isn't your call."

"I think we've already figured out who'll win this fight." Breaking his hold, I push him off. "She thinks she can trust him. I won't let her get hurt."

"She won't," he insists. "Would you rather her be out there alone?"

I grit my teeth. "Knowing the fucking UNSUB is one of you? Yeah. I'd say she's safer being on her own."

Carson keeps my glare, neither of us making a move until he turns his head away, distracted. He presses a finger to his ear. "They got a hit on the DNA," he says.

My whole body comes alive. I'm off the wall, muscles thrumming with the need to *move*. "Who is he?" There's still time. They can pull Sadie out. *I* can pull Sadie out.

Carson shakes his head. "They're not saying. They're

running facial recognition software on everyone in the club. Fucking FBI. That will take forever, and they're looking in the wrong damn place."

"Who is he?" I'm seconds away from coming out of my skin.

Carson finally meets my gaze. "I don't know. But he must be big on the inside if they're keeping that on lock down. Just calm down. We'll get ahold of Sadie." He looks around, then throws his hands up. "Shit. She doesn't have a phone."

But she does. I head back into the voyeur and locate the landline phone behind the bar. My thumbs push the numbers I memorized, my heart beating painfully against my chest wall. On the fifth ring, it goes to voicemail. No recording. Just a generic beep.

My fist locks around the phone, ready to pound the information from Carson's mouth with the damn earpiece, but to hell with that. My feet are already moving, taking me past him and down the hallway, then down the stairs. I don't stop as I clear a path toward the exit.

I throw the side door open and break into a run, heading right for the not-so-discreet van parked a block away. I hear Carson calling my name, but I can't slow.

Before I reach the van, two FBI agents apprehend me. "She's not in there...neither is your UNSUB. Sadie's out there—"

"Sir, you have to calm down," one of them says. He

tilts his chin toward his shoulder. "Sir, we have a situation here."

The van door opens, and out comes Agent Proctor, the head honcho who took over my club. "Colton Reed. I figured we'd have a problem with you."

The agents drag me into the van. Proctor grabs me by the neck. "I told them not to let a civilian in on this op," he says. "Cuff him. Reed, you're being arrested for obstruction."

"I don't give a damn. You're wasting your time trying to find him inside the club. He's not there."

Proctor squints his pale eyes at me. "What are you talking about?"

"Sir." An agent sitting before a row of monitors turns our way. "We have another situation."

"Son of a bitch." Proctor scrubs a hand down his face. "What is it?"

"Agent Bonds, sir. She's missing."

Proctor turns and points to one of the monitors, to where the UC agent is still sitting at Sadie's table. "Then who the hell is that?"

"I don't know, sir. But she's not Agent Bonds. We ran facial recognition for Agent Bonds, also…to try to locate the perp, assuming he would be near her. We were trying to narrow the search parameters—"

"Jesus Christ, spit it out!" Proctor shouts.

"The program confirmed Agent Bonds isn't inside the club, sir."

Proctor says into his radio, "Detective Carson, bring that decoy agent here. I'm going to have everyone's badges before the end of the night." Then he narrows his gaze on me. "Where is she? Where's Bonds?"

My throat burns dry. "I don't know, but Quinn does. Locate him. Do whatever you do to track him. He's out there with her."

I know I'm breaking my promise to Sadie…but as soon as I heard Quinn changed the game plan, I could feel it in my bones—sense the tables turning. Sadie's in danger.

And as soon as my words register with Proctor, I see it in his eyes, too.

Proctor brings his radio up. "Pull everyone out!" He turns to the front of the van. "Get the coordinates up on Quinn's last known location. I want eyes on this perp now."

YOU

SADIE

"**T**hat little fucker!" Quinn slurs.

I brace my hand underneath his head, bringing him into my lap. "Don't move. Where's your radio?" My hands shake with adrenaline, my head pounds with the rapid beat of my pulse.

I rip a section of my dress and tear it free, then wipe the blood from Quinn's lips. "Jesus, Quinn. What are you doing here? What happened?"

He tries to sit up and falls backward, grabs the back of his head. "I was tailing you," he admits. "Don't look at me like that." He turns his head away and spits out the blood filling his mouth.

"You botched it," I say, my jaw tight. I push him aside and get to my feet, bending over to grab Quinn's radio. He intercepts it first. "Avery's life depended on this, Quinn." Then it hits me." He knew. He *knew* that I wouldn't be alone. Whatever plan you had going, he knew beforehand." I think about the necklace—coated in blood—and anger fuels my limbs so swiftly I have to grip my hair to keep from screaming.

Sitting forward, he says, "I know. I fucked up. But dammit, Bonds…I wasn't going to lose you." He stares up at me, and I see the pain he's in. Mentally and physically. My anger dissipates. But only a fraction.

"What happened?" I demand.

He opens his mouth and touches his jaw, rocks it back and forth. "My tooth is gone."

Bile coats my throat. "…What?"

"I was jumped from behind and hit over the head ." He groans as he touches the back of his head. "I came to with fucking pliers in my mouth. He ripped my damn tooth out." He glances at me. "But I got a good hit in. I think we can pull some trace. Maybe even blood." He looks over his knuckles.

"This doesn't make sense," I say, shaking my head. "It couldn't have been the UNSUB."

Quinn raises his eyebrows and stares up at me. "Who the hell would it have been? How many other psychopaths did we lure here who would rip my fucking tooth out? I'm sure he wasn't done with me."

The honesty of that statement smacks me hard. No,

Quinn would be missing much more than his tooth if the perpetrator would've had time. "Can you ID him?"

He shakes his head, then winces. "Too dark. But think about it. It was personal." Quinn leans over to spit again. "Only someone within the department would know about my damn tooth. My personal brand of torture. Crazy dentists," he says, trying to diminish the severity of his injuries.

Quinn's radio crackles. "The perp is on foot. Repeat. The perp is on foot. All units be advised. White male, approximately six foot, brown hair and wearing black clothing was last scene leaving TRI."

Quinn wipes his mouth using the scrap of my dress to clean the blood away. He lifts the radio. "Kyle, do you have his location?"

Static. "Negative."

Quinn curses.

Flashes of red and blue light up the highway, blinking against the wooded tree line. I pull Quinn's arm over my shoulder and help him stand as unis surround the memorial. Once I'm sure Quinn can stand without my support, I step away and take out Colton's phone.

I'm dialing the number to the club when I spot Colton entering the clearing. In cuffs. Being escorted by Carson. "Get those off him," I shout.

I make a beeline for Colton, but Proctor steps into my path. "This will go down as the worst UC operation ever. I hope you have a good explanation, and a damn good reason as to why I shouldn't lock every single one of you up for obstruction."

"Quinn needs medical attention," I say, nodding to where he's sitting on one of the benches. "I take full responsibility. I put Quinn in harm's way. I organized a side op to apprehend the UNSUB away from the club."

"And failed. Big time," Proctor grates. He points toward the bridge. "You and your crew. In the van for debriefing."

I glance back at Quinn, a mix of emotions assaulting me. Anger that he didn't trust me enough to enter the field on my own battling with my concern for him. He almost got himself killed.

"He'll live." Proctor eyes me closely before he shakes his head and starts toward Quinn. "It will be your captain who takes the hit. Just remember that."

People know just where to strike to hurt the worst. No one else was supposed to suffer for this. And now...now, we've loosed an unstable psychopath on Avery. She'll pay the highest price.

I turn toward Carson. "Uncuff him."

He expels a heavy breath. "Why not? I've already lost my badge. Why not go the whole nine yards and let the Feds arrest me, too." He jerks his head toward the bridge. "Not here."

As we make our way toward the van, I link my arm through Colton's. "How did you end up arrested?"

"I ratted you out."

I stop short. Turning to face him fully, I say, "You did what?"

Carson holds up his hand. "It doesn't matter, Sadie. The Feds already made the UC agent. The op was a bust as soon as they got a hit on the DNA from the sample."

My head begins to spin. Despite being cuffed, Colton manages to keep me upright. I lean into his chest. "We have the UNSUB?"

Carson's features smooth some. "Yeah. Well, we have his identity. You know that lab tech that works with Avery? The tall guy. Glasses. Skinny…"

My stomach bottoms out. "Simon?"

"Simon Whitmore. He evaded the initial search of the department by tampering with his file. That's why the profile didn't align with him," Carson says. "The Feds have already pulled his original info. He worked in the Roanoke forensic lab. Moved here about six months ago, though his file states he's been here for a year after transferring from upstate."

I take off toward the Van.

If Avery isn't already dead…if there's a chance she's still alive…finding that bastard Simon is our only hope. I pull the door open and am immersed in a full-scale search already in progress.

One monitor displays Simon Whitmore, his face captioned as the UNSUB—the face I looked right into as he handed me the note from Avery. The techs are running searches on his financials, a team already en route to his house and two hotels that he recently paid for with a credit card.

"He won't be in a hotel," I say, climbing into the van. "And he won't have Avery at his house. You need to take the search back further, to places he visited six months ago."

Agent Rollins snaps his fingers. "Get her out of here," he orders one of the agents.

"Proctor sent me," I say, jerking my arm free of the agent's grip. "I'm to be debriefed, and there's no way you're shutting me out if there's a chance our M.E. is still alive."

I hear Carson and Colton enter the van, and Agent Rollins slams his hand against the wall. "You amateurs have already botched things good enough. What? You want to see if we can get the perp off on a technicality, too?"

"Can I leave?"

Our heads swing toward the woman hired to be my double.

Rollins glares at her. "Not unless you want the full weight of your charges brought against you. Sit down."

She rolls her eyes with exaggeration, and Carson takes it upon himself to lead her toward the back of the van.

"Did she ID him?" I ask Rollins.

"She did," he says, crossing his arms over his chest. "She confirms Simon Whitmore, a tech from your own department lab, hired her to dance with him at the club and lead Reed out the side entrance. She claims she doesn't know anything else. But she's going into interrogation just to be sure."

The UNSUB has been on a mission today, closing up loose ends. Why not her?

"You wouldn't have half the information you do now without us putting our lives on the line," I say, turning my back to him and moving closer to the monitors. "You will give us the respect we're due, and you will either work with us now to help our M.E., or you can get the fuck out of the way."

The air of the van thickens with tension. I can feel Rollins simmering, his close proximity hovering behind me. I'm sure he's about to have me escorted from the vehicle when he says, "I better not regret this, Agent Bonds."

He has one of the analysts bring up Simon's financial records for the past six months. "See if you can find a recurring payment on property—rent, mortgage, or it might even be disguised as a car payment. Go back further into his records and see if he inherited any property. Any gifts he tried to get past the IRS."

Carson appears at the head of the van. "He's not what I expected," he says. "I feel almost…disappointed."

This is true. Simon Whitmore is a shadow. He was easy to overlook because nothing about him stood out. Average looks. Average height. Average life. He's so unassuming that no one would bother to look too closely… if they ever bothered to notice him at all.

"You've had an ideal suspect in mind for two years," I say to Carson. "It's hard to imagine anyone outside that profile once you've made up your mind."

Our gazes connect briefly, letting an unsaid understanding pass between us out of respect for Colton. Julian couldn't be the apprentice. He was too much of an alpha to ever submit to anyone else.

I look at Rollins. "We need to compare the evidence of the crime scenes to this knew information."

Rollins tosses a pile of files down on the table in the center of the van. "Knock yourselves out."

Feeling like this night is about to swallow me, I take up a seat next to Colton, the weight of this day finally catching up. I tweak a file from the stack and flip it open.

My vision blurs. I blink hard, trying to focus on the crime scene image from the suspended vic. It was what Avery was last working on. There has to be something here I missed. It's the only scene where a mistake was made—one he caught, but just barely. He was devolving rapidly at this point; he could've made another mistake.

"I'm sorry, goddess," Colton whispers near my ear.

My insides hum. Just hearing him say *goddess* takes me away from the cruel reality gripping my mind. "You don't have to be," I say. "I never would've let you go."

His jaw clenches. "I almost didn't…I was close to locking you up in my room."

I smile. For him. "I promised you we would get through this." I look into his eyes. "Why did you—?"

"I thought Quinn was the UNSUB."

I huff a weak laugh. "He couldn't be. Well, I might've questioned him at one point. He went through a rough divorce a few months ago; that's enough of a trigger for anyone to commit homicide. And he's a neat freak. I cut my eyes a few times at him with suspicion...but no." I shake my head. "Quinn isn't subservient enough. Also, he didn't spend enough time in Roanoke to build a connection with Connelly. If anything, Quinn would be the master, not the apprentice."

Colton's eyes skim my face, then travel lower as he lifts the tattered hem of my dress. "When I first saw you... all I could imagine was Quinn attacking you. Or someone hurting you. I learned the hard way you can't break out of handcuffs."

I take his hand in mine and run my fingers over the bloody welts around his wrist. "I'm sorry I put you through this." I swallow hard. "Quinn was attacked. Not me."

"I wouldn't put it past Quinn to fake an attack. To throw suspicion off of him."

"I doubt Quinn would've pulled his own tooth," I say, returning my gaze to the crime scene image. "He won't go anywhere near dentists. He's squeamish about anything that has to do with them."

Colton stares at the image from over my shoulder. "I

don't understand why he'd use a bowline knot to hoist the victim," he says suddenly.

My head jerks up. "What?"

"At this crime scene. He tied a bowline knot." He gets closer to me to whisper. "If it were me, I'd use a blood knot. Ten times as strong, better to support a body, and it's more poetic. Keeping to the theme of the Blood Countess."

I turn my gaze on him. "Who would use a bowline knot?"

He shrugs. "It's a basic knot. Easy to learn. So really anyone. But you mostly see it used on boats. Like sailboats."

A surge of hope springs me to my feet. "See if Simon has access to a boat. No wait… Pull up Lyle Connelly's financials and look for—"

"I have it," the tech says. "There was a title transfer between Connelly and Whitmore five months ago. A sailboat was gifted to Whitmore. To avoid paying taxes, Connelly's lawyer drew up the paperwork in a charity's name registered through Whitmore."

I'm back at the front, staring at the screen as if I can find Simon on the map. Proctor stands beside me. "Bring up every boat slip between Arlington and DC. He might not have it registered in his name. Crosscheck the slips and the names of the boats."

"I found one, sir." The tech transfers the data from one screen to another, zooming in on an aerial view of the

Columbia Island Marina. "The Countess. It's docked at the marina now."

"That's just a few minutes away." Quinn's voice comes from behind.

I whip around. "Am I removed from the field?"

He frowns. "Could I order you to stay put?"

"Not a chance."

THE COUNTESS

SADIE

My necklace rests safely in the pocket of my hoodie. There's a tiny glimmer of optimism sparking within me that Avery is still alive—and I don't want to corrupt that hope, that *faith*. Normally, I don't give in to superstition. But I feel like as long as I don't show anyone…if no one actually sees the proof of her blood…then it won't come true.

Since the attack on Quinn at TRI, the UNSUB has gone silent. He's sent no communication to me about Avery's condition. And one piece of evidence in the form of Simon's DNA has granted us a warrant to search his sailboat with strict parameters to locate Avery there.

It's the most logical place as to where she's being kept.

The Feds have taken the lead on this assignment. After

Proctor thoroughly reamed Quinn for my side op, he almost benched Quinn and the whole task force for our blatant disregard of protocol. But seeing as they need our numbers to make a clean collar of Simon Whitmore, and to assure the operation goes down safely, it was in his best interest to let us "tag along."

I don't care about the bureaucracy. I've never been concerned with politics. And quite frankly, I went into this field knowing my ethics were questionable. You don't come out of the other side of a dark moment in time to the light. It doesn't conclude on a fairytale ending. Prince Charming doesn't swoop in and save the damsel in distress. The heroine doesn't suddenly experience a life-altering realization that she can conquer her demons and become a beacon—a role model for all suffering souls to follow in her footsteps…

This is not that story.

My abductor will forever taint my reality. The nightmares will live on inside my soul, and I will cry out in the middle of the night. Though there is now someone there to wrap his arms around me when the dreams claw me back down to the dungeon, they will never truly cease to exist within me.

And now, through me, because I have altered a moment in time through my own lingering, haunting darkness, another soul has been touched. Avery will never truly overcome this. She will search for someone to hold her in the night, and she will seek acceptance for her altered reality not only from herself, but from everyone she comes into contact with in the future.

We'll share a similar but silent bond—we'll look into each other's eyes and know: *we're the same.* But we will never talk about it. Not to the depths or extent that it has irrevocably impacted our lives.

This is our secret world.

My thoughts drift away, back into the abyss, as Quinn takes up the front. We're pressed against the marina's facility building, our backs to the brick. The Pentagon sits just across the harbor. To get here unnoticed, we had to move in small groups. The first group is headed up by Proctor and closest to The Countess. Proctor got a warrant to commandeer Simon's neighboring sailboat; the owner's of that vessel are being kept at the station out of harm's way.

Four FBI agents are aboard the vessel now.

Quinn taps at his earpiece. "There's movement on The Countess. Proctor's going in with the first group." He glances over his shoulder. "When we move in, watch your six."

I nod. I want to be the one to look Simon in his eyes when he sees his end coming. When the knowledge that he won't ever advance to "master" first lights his eyes. But I'll settle for looking into them during the aftermath.

I just hope they don't have to kill him before I get that chance.

A crackle sounds through my own earpiece, and my

muscles tense, my grip on my gun tightens. Quinn is first in command for our small group of three. Just me, Quinn, and Carson. I could almost laugh that it's come down to this—stuck between two men that only a week ago, I almost pegged for accomplices.

Carson and Quinn would've made an interesting team —but truthfully, I'm not sure who would be the master, and who would be the apprentice. They're both too stubborn to take clear directives from the other. Though I give Carson credit, he does try awfully hard to impress Quinn.

My train of thought stops suddenly as a shout comes through my feed. *Hands up! Hands up!* Then the rest happens too quickly for me to distinguish.

A shot rings out…my heart slams against my chest, my foot digs into the earth…and the order to move in sounds through the earpiece. Quinn throws his hand forward, ordering us to advance.

The earth moves up and down in my vision. The thud of footfalls bounces heavy in my ears. An out-of-body euphoria washes over me. And for one, clear second, I take notice of the moonlit river. The reflection of the luminescent orb shimmering and reflecting off tranquil waters.

The Countess is a large sailboat. I note this also, along with the rocking of the boat. Something this massive shouldn't stir so easily as we board the vessel.

"Fall back!" Proctor stands with his gun hiked to his

shoulder, giving orders. "The suspect is down. Group two, search the rest of the cabin. Apprehend anyone else on this vessel."

I hear the order. I'm following Quinn's lead as he heads below into the hull, Carson right behind me. But my eyes are taking in everything—trying to understand why they haven't seen Avery yet.

"Quinn—"

"We'll find her," he says.

The deeper we go into the cabin, the darker it becomes. The thicker the air settles around us. It's like going underground, the feel of entering a tomb. A coldness bites into my skin, and I clamp both hands around my SIG for comfort.

The noise above becomes a muffled annoyance. I realize the walls are covered with padding. This is familiar; my abductor did the same to his basement. As we descend, the steps creaking beneath our feet, one sound— one beautiful sound—catches my ears.

A whimper.

It's the sound of terror—but it's lovely. It's the sound I made when Jackson Randall Lovett was shot to death beside me, and I looked into the beams of the flashlights, right into the barrels of the guns. And then into the eyes of the FBI agents.

Avery is making that sound now.

"Clear the room," Quinn orders. "Cover everywhere."

It's an impossible directive to follow when all I want to

do is rush to Avery—but this time, I follow the order. Enough rules have been broken. I need to stay the course to make sure she survives this.

"Clear!" Carson shouts.

"Clear here, too," Quinn says from the corner of the dungeon.

Because that's what this is. A verified hell in the belly of a ship.

I finish checking my corner, forcing my fingers to ease off the handle of my gun. "Clear." Only I'm not so sure…

Along one wall, in beautiful script: *She walks in beauty, like the night…*

And on the opposite wall: *Her walls talk…*

The next wall displays another verse from the dreaded poem: *Had half impaired the nameless grace… Which waves in every* raven *tress*

And above Avery, written in perfect penmanship: *We are all apprentices in a craft where no one ever becomes a master.*

The final clue—a quote from Ernest Hemingway. How poetic.

I release a lengthy breath and meet Quinn's eyes. He nods once, giving me permission, and I don't hesitate. I holster my gun and drop down beside Avery.

"It's okay," I assure her. My arms link her bare shoulders. The red dress has been mutilated. I can feel the welts covering her skin against my arms. Her body shakes, tremors and I'm sure sheer exhaustion wracking her limbs. "Shh…" I soothe. "Avery, it's going to be okay."

I continue to repeat reassurances to her as the EMTs enter the hull. Carson has located bolt cutters and proceeds to cut her chains away at the go-ahead from one of the EMTs.

Her body is broken. Her mind isn't fairing any better. Her once vibrant brown irises are glazed and refuse to make contact with mine. She hasn't looked up from the floor once to acknowledge anyone. She's been staring at the ground for so long, beaten and trained to stare at it— and she's in shock.

But she's alive.

This is not her fairytale ending.

She won't spring to her feet and whoop for joy to her saviors, like they do in the movies. She won't even cry tears of relief. She will tremble and puke and roil in the sickness until the medics clear her to be given a sedative where she can sleep off the shock.

For once, I wish she could experience just one more thing of mine. I wish he was killed right before her. I fear she will never be able to go into a dark room, or turn off the lights in her lab to inspect evidence, without the fear of him finding her again.

And so that's what I offer her.

As I follow the EMTs escorting Avery toward the deck level of the boat, I clasp her hand, squeeze tightly until her head whips around and her eyes finally see—really *see* —mine.

Against protocol, I pull her away and toward the dead man being photographed on the ship's floor. "Look at him," I say to her as I kneel down and tear his mask away. "Imprint him into your memory."

For just a moment, as her gaze takes in his limp body, her shivers subside. Then, turning to me, she says, "Thank you."

It's past midnight, and the hospital is still catering to the ACPD. Lukewarm coffee and donuts have been brought in by the unis. Prayers have been uttered in the hallways. Nurses offer weak but reassuring smiles to the cops littering the waiting room.

Avery deserves all the encouragement. No one has been able to see her, which is for the best. She's not ready. But she will appreciate so many of her fellow crime fighters offering their support. When she's ready.

I sit with my back up against the cool wall, savoring the quiet. In this wing of the hospital, it's slow and dim. An overhead light is blown, and my eyes desperately need a break from the fluorescents.

I don't know when I shut my eyes, but they pop open

at the feel of a cup slipping between my hands. It's warm…much warmer than the weak coffee I had earlier. I take a sip. "Thanks."

Quinn slips down on the floor beside me. "I almost didn't wake you, but you looked too comfortable."

I smile. "That's a bad thing, apparently."

"Terrible." He brings his own coffee up and takes a long sip. "So they found my tooth in Simon's pocket."

"You going to get it back?"

"Funny." He glances at me. "Obviously, it's going into an evidence locker where it will rot."

I shrug against the wall. "Too bad. We could've given it a proper burial. I know how you'll miss it."

"Smart ass."

Silence settles between us as we drink our coffee. As the discomfort of it stretches out, my chest tightens. "I need to see my mother, and Colton…before you bring me in," I say, breaking the quiet.

He runs his palms along his slacks, wiping away the creases. Even now, he has to keep things in order. "I've made a decision on that," he says, continuing to rub at nonexistent wrinkles. "I just came from my debriefing. Proctor had a pile of paperwork for me."

I turn to look at him. "He couldn't cut you some slack tonight?"

He huffs a laugh. "You'd think. But no, there was still the matter of Connelly's death to close out."

My breath stills in my chest.

"Connelly was reported missing. Body never found. After the night you told me to look into him, I reopened the investigation into his disappearance." Quinn's gaze remains steady on the linoleum floor.

I grip the cup. Ready. "You need a statement from me," I say. "All right. I'll follow you to the department. Let's make it official."

He sighs. "Apparently, the Feds never closed their investigation on him. When they first showed up, I thought it was my interest in the case that brought them here. That I'd set off some red flags…and I was terrified, Bonds." He looks at me then. "For you. That's not how I wanted it to go down."

Confusion mars my face. "Because you want to bring me in."

He expels a silent curse. "Do you really think I want to see my partner brought down by the Feds?"

"Then what are you saying, Quinn?"

He relieves me of my coffee, sets it on the floor. Looks into my eyes. "They did a thorough search of Simon's boat and found journals. He liked to record things. And one of those things was how he did away with his mentor. He even noted where he burned the body."

My heart flutters wildly, my pulse slamming against my veins. "That's impossible. That doesn't fit his profile. At all. He wouldn't be capable of killing his master—"

"Proctor wanted me to sign off on the case. I did. The case is closed. They're still going to inspect the scene, look

210

for any trace of Connelly's remains...but it's highly unlikely anything will be uncovered by this point."

I swallow the hard lump in my throat. "But...you know it isn't true. You know—"

Quinn presses a finger over my mouth. My whole body freezes. His eyes bore into mine as he says, "*I* don't know anything."

He holds my gaze for a moment longer, then drops his hand as he rises and walks away.

I stare after him. At my partner.

THE STILL, DARK HAUNTS

COLTON

I finish stuffing another box full of Julian's suits. Bethany wanted me to take them, said they'd look good on me, that Julian would want me to have them—but I don't need my brother's tailored suits to remember him by.

Besides, they wouldn't look good on me.

They're going to be donated to one of his many charities. This time, for real. My brother had a lot of bogus charity contributions as a cover to shuffle around his money. It seems fitting that as his final act he should honor them with his most prized possession. His damn suits.

During the funeral yesterday, I was worried about the mix of people. The one thing I'm sure my brother cared about was Bethany. Whatever double life he was leading behind her back is over now. So she shouldn't have to suffer that discovery on top of his death. But just like their engagement party, where my brother was able to pull off his double life, seems even from the grave he's full of swagger. The wake went just as smoothly.

I tape up the last box and toss it into the hallway. At least doing this for Bethany makes me feel a little less shitty. I still don't know why the UNSUB—or Simon—killed Julian. Why he felt my brother was a threat that needed to be eliminated. My brother's only crime was in knowing I ended Marni's life. That I staged her crime scene to pin it on a serial killer.

I know it was Julian who deleted the club surveillance footage—the footage the analysts were never able to recover. I just don't know why he did it. And now, I'll never know.

Sadie has a theory. It's as good as any. She thinks the UNSUB was allowing Julian to blackmail him in order to have access to the club. Simon proved to be a member of The Lair. He used a pseudonym and his member profile was completely phony; it was so vanilla and unassuming that I skipped right past him during my search.

That still pisses me off—that I couldn't recognize a psychopathic sadist in my own club. But truthfully, Julian conducted all the interviews. It was most likely during that exchange when an agreement was reached between them.

I've battled the past three days with wanting to know…and wanting to forget.

My brother knew the cops were looking at the club. He knew the killer was possibly a member. If Julian figured out who he was…then it's logical the UNSUB needed to get rid of him.

It's clean. It puts all doubts away. I try to let that be my answer.

Most of the time, I'm able to accept it. The Feds and the ACPD, and hell, even Carson accepts it—that should be reason enough for me. And I like the idea that my brother was attempting to do the right thing in the end. That maybe, just maybe, he wasn't trying to delete that footage… That he was trying to copy it to send to the cops.

I force out a breath and wipe my hands off on a rag, officially done.

I'm done.

Taking another glance around my brother's home, saying my last goodbye, I head downstairs.

"You're off?"

I turn to see Bethany in the living room, a small box in her hands.

"I'm done, so yeah. I have to finish up signing some documents with his lawyer. Figured I'd go take care of that now." The documents which officially make me the owner of The Lair. The process was already started before his death; this will just make it legit.

She smiles. "Well, thank you. I appreciate the help. It's been hard trying to go through his stuff…" She trails off, shakes her head. "Anyway. Julian had a box of memorabilia. I could never get him to throw it out." She laughs. "He was such a packrat. I thought you'd like to have it."

I hold up my hand, about to refuse, but she says, "Please, Colton. I know he'd want you to have it."

I accept the box with a tight smile. My final act as Julian's brother.

I spring awake, my heart galloping in my chest.

The AC blasts my sweat-slicked skin, the covers a tangled mess around my ankles. I wipe a hand down my face, clearing the burning sweat from my eyes.

The pitch black plays tricks on my mind…and just for a second…I think I see Sadie standing at the foot of the bed.

I reach over and switch on the lamp. Her jean jacket hangs on the coat hanger along the wall. I lie back and roll over, reaching out to pull her close, but my hand grasps at empty space.

"Sadie?"

My voice sounds odd in her bedroom. I'm not used to sleeping at her apartment yet. But since Avery's rescue, she's been too high strung to sleep at mine, not wanting to upset my roommate Jefferson every time she screams out in the night.

It's the first time I've awoken before the screaming starts.

Throwing my legs over the edge of the bed, I push onto my feet and head to the bathroom. The nightlight illuminates my shadowy reflection in the mirror. I can see the pallor of my complexion, enhanced by the dim, blue light.

After I relieve myself, my brain is awake and functional. I search for Sadie in the living room, the kitchen, her office. The laptop is on. I can't stop the dread climbing up my spine. I grab my phone and call her. No answer. I send her a text.

Me: *Where are you, goddess?*

I wait, hoping to see the three little dots that signify she's typing back—but they never appear.

She's at the department. Some call came in, and fucking Quinn couldn't let it wait till morning. That's what my brain wants to believe…but the nagging suspicion that something's wrong won't let me. Not fully.

I've watched her for three days. Three furious days full of events. The funeral. The wake. Avery's recovery. Further investigation into Simon Whitmore. It's been

217

nonstop—and all through it, I've watched Sadie. Calm. Collected. Removed.

But I know she's been through this before; she's been through far worse. Distancing herself is a defense mechanism. She has old wounds to protect.

I sit down in her office chair and my gaze lands on Julian's box. I rip the tape off and flip the cardboard flaps open. A framed photo of me, Julian, and Marni stares back at me. It was taken one night at the bar we frequented. It was taken before Julian and I had the fight. Before Marni was diagnosed with cancer.

I set it on the desk and dig through the other contents of the box. All stuff that wouldn't mean much to anyone other than Julian. Baseball cards from when he was a kid. His piggy bank. A laugh escapes me. I take out the porcelain bank, an actual fat pig that he cherished. It was his first practice into the art of blackmail.

You'd think with how he valued money, he'd have actually used it for that purpose. But even then, even as a kid, Julian understood that secrets were a cash commodity. He used to hide little notes inside; things he caught people doing. My dad sneaking a porno mag in with the groceries. Stupid shit like that.

I forgot all about it until now. I lift the bank out and hear a tinker. I shake it, then uncork the bottom. A USB drive falls into my lap.

With a sick twist in the pit of my stomach, I grab the

drive. I don't have to look at what's on it; I already know. And if I do look…there's no going back. That reality where my brother was the good guy in his final moments will be shattered. I was willing to let it ride—I spent two years hating him, blaming him. I should let it ride.

But my hand is already finding the USB port on the side of Sadie's laptop. The drive is already booting up. The file pops open on the screen, revealing months of labeled footage.

I click open the top file. My brother's image inside the club is clear and present. The timestamp denotes it's about an hour before Carson and I showed up. Julian walks right through the club. But when he reaches the office door, he looks up at the hallway camera…and waves. The footage cuts off shortly after he goes inside.

Icy fingers trail my back.

I skip down to the night the UNSUB sent me a pic of Sadie in the club. It's timestamped and labeled: Sadie and Wells.

My hand hovers over the mouse pad, my fingers trembling. Either with fear or hesitation, it's the same. But I click the file and start the footage.

For a few minutes, everything looks normal. Nothing out of the ordinary happens. Sadie watches the stage, glancing over her shoulder toward the entryway every couple of minutes. She's waiting for me. The sickness takes hold when I see *him*.

Standing at the bar, watching her.

I've seen him before.

He lifts his phone in her direction. There. Right there. The image that was sent to me. *He* sent it. And fucking Julian knew... Why the hell didn't he tell me?

There's footage of this guy all over the file. All labeled: Watcher Wells.

With adrenaline pumping, I close the footage and open the file dated for the first night I spoke to Sadie. Our very first conversation, when I finally found an opening to approach her.

I thought I was taking advantage of that moment. There was an asshole in a business suit hitting on her...and it was the perfect instance to meet her. No one could have planned a better chance encounter.

But he did.

I watch as the scene plays out. The guy in the dark gray business suit walking up to Sadie. Her demeanor changing, becoming withdrawn. Me leaning against the wall, watching them. When he bends down and touches her...then pulls her against him...that's when I act.

What did he say?

"She wants it. She's just shy... She needs a little persuading."

And in his own demented way, he's been trying to persuade her ever since, the sick shit. I accused him of not watching her. Of not understanding what she needed. Of not knowing that she hates being touched.

He knew it all.

Watcher Wells. Mother fucker. He'd been stalking her the whole damn time.

It happened so quickly.

I never thought about that guy again. Not once.

The bad apple.

MASTER

SADIE

The alleyway is damp and chilly. Fall grips the air, letting us know winter's presence is inevitable. The storm that blew through left behind a frigid reminder that we're all susceptible to the cold and dark nights.

My heels *clack* against the pavement. The echo being drowned out by the thump of bass the closer I get. I turn a corner and music bleeds into the street—an invitation to enter the only nightlife along this strip of the city.

So I do. I walk through the doors of the bar, where just above a neon sign blazes: Raven.

It's a small bar. Trendy. Only a handful of two-seater tables, one pool table, and a long stretch of cherry oak bar top that wraps toward the back wall. That's where I sit; the far corner where I can see the front door, the one leading to a single bathroom, and the scope of the room.

As the bartender approaches, a man with a beard and stretched earlobes, I order my pink champagne, having to shout over the music. He raises an eyebrow, but doesn't mock my choice. I stare at the door, absentmindedly fingering the crest dangling from my neck.

A clatter draws my attention, and I whip around as someone whoops. Billiard balls bounce around the black felt, and I watch three sink home into the corner pockets.

"Ma'am."

I swivel back around to find the bartender eyeing me. He sets the flute down, then slides a tumbler my way. "SoCo on the rocks."

The nape of my neck tingles; the tiny hairs lifting away from my skin.

"I didn't order that," I say.

He tries to smooth it over with a smile. "No, ma'am. The gentleman at that table did." He nods toward the opposite corner.

I don't turn to look. Accepting my drinks with a corresponding smile, I pick up both the flute and the tumbler. Then I scoot off the barstool, my feet sure and my back straight as I pivot and saunter toward the table.

"Enjoying his drink is a little tacky, don't you think?"

The man in the gray business suit drags his gaze over me. From my legs, up my red dress, to the necklace, meeting my eyes. A crooked smile hikes the corner of his mouth, jogging my memory. It's the same knowing smirk he gave me that night in the club.

"It can't be in bad taste if we enjoy it, now can it?" he says, his voice a mix of dark seduction and farce. "Have a seat. Please. I beg of you."

I don't approve of having my back to an open room, but considering the company, it's best to keep my undivided attention on him. I set my drinks down and take the seat across the table from the UNSUB—who is no longer an unknown subject.

This secluded section gives us enough privacy, while being a good distance from the bar speakers so we can hear clearly, but our voices don't carry to the other patrons. He chose well.

I drink from the tumbler, deciding that it's about time I sample what Connelly favored, before I steeple my hands over the drink. "I feel as if introductions are a little late, but just the same…" I say, prompting him.

He crooks another smile at me. "Our given names are so trivial. But if my lady must know, I go by Price Alexander Wells." His finger traces the tumbler before him as his dark eyes dance over my skin. "Lawyer by day, outlaw by night." His smile dims when his poor joke gets no result. He clears his throat. "You have to forgive me. I'm somewhat nervous. See, this is a big moment for me."

"Me, too," I indulge him.

His smile returns.

"So, a lawyer," I say, running my finger over the rim of

the glass. "You wouldn't happen to be Connelly's lawyer. The same lawyer that transferred the title of his sailboat into Simon's name."

"Nothing slips past you." He takes a sip of his drink. "Connelly thought it'd be a good idea to have a lawyer in his pocket. I guess, more than anything, that's why he chose me. I used to flatter myself that there were other, more notable reasons. But when it comes right down to it, people are selfish beasts."

"We are," I agree.

He sits forward. "I hate to ask…because fishing *is* in such poor taste…but did you enjoy my gifts?"

A sharp pain hitches my breathing. The press of a blade against my thigh helps me swallow the yelp clawing up my throat, and I still the squirm traveling over me. "To answer that question truthfully, yes. At least, a part of me enjoyed them."

His eyes darken. "I had hoped they wouldn't be a disappointment. That by now, you'd realize that's the only part that matters."

The blade is gone within the same beat that he pushes back in his chair, giving me the space I need to present my case. I drink my champagne. All of it.

Then, "There are two antisocial dispositions"—I narrow my gaze—"psychopaths and sociopaths. Those who are born, and those who are forged."

He clips a light laugh. "Battle of wills, is it?"

I nod slowly.

Arrogantly—as I anticipated he would be—he reaches across the table and steals my tumbler. His eyes drill into me as he tips the SoCo to his mouth. Then he returns the drink to me. "I always take what I want. I have since birth. So I suppose that means I was born to it," he says effortlessly.

"And I was created."

"The difference?"

The difference? Is there a difference when it comes right down to it? Until Colton found me, I thought I was incapable of feeling. Of empathy. After my captor broke me down to my barest attributes, I saw just how similar I was to him—how when stripped of all the things we think matter, everything we believe defines us, we're all just creatures who will hurt, kill, deceive...who will do anything to survive. But not just survive: *thrive*.

The lesson my captor taught me was this: destroy or be destroyed.

Pain doesn't always stem from those who intend us harm. It can come from the ones we trust the most. A parent—a well-meaning parent who, trying her best to shelter her child, suffocates them. A lover who believes he's helping you overcome your pain, but inflicts it upon you in the process. Because he loves you so deeply...he can't live without you. His codependency becomes your guilt.

I was never so disillusioned. My captor relieved me of that deception. I knew all too well how easy it was to slip from one side of the spectrum to the other, all in the name of love. Feelings. Emotions.

I was thankful to my captor for removing the burden of having to balance on that precise emotional edge of right and wrong.

That's why, I think, during those early years where I searched desperately for an answer to someone like me, I found a connection in Elizabeth Bathory. She, too, was created. She, too, had to have experienced some immeasurable suffering that cast her in the design of a monster. She, too, couldn't help but seek out a source to funnel her pain.

I believe she saw something of herself—something she envied or lost—in the girls she killed. Maybe she envied their carefree childhood. Maybe I identify with her there— my own having been stolen away. But ultimately, it's not why I formed a bond with the Countess.

Uncovering my own historic relation to Bathory sealed my resolve.

Once I understood my lineage, I transformed myself into a stalker of stalkers. A killer of killers. I would not wait for the broken and devastated souls to come to me; I would seek out their tormenters and punish them for their life-destroying sins.

Born or forged? With a bloodline linked to one of the most infamous serial killers of the millennia, does it matter? I could've just as easily been born defective.

Only I wasn't. I was created. Colton proved this to me,

showing me that I can cure the raging demon within. That it's not pain that feeds the beast; it's the depth of our love that quiets it.

Killing the thing I'm most terrified of becoming is no longer my calling. Though I'm sure there will be times when it's the only answer, I can *choose*. I can determine who is worthy. I am not bound to deliver the monster's bidding at its mercy.

Connelly was not my first, nor will he be the last. But he's somehow the one who called my reckoning. For that, I am humbled.

So, is there a difference?

"Yes," I say with absolute certainty. "The difference between you and I is that I am distinct in my defect, by which I have a choice." At his confused expression, I continue, "You can't help the monster you are, Price. You have to snuff out the threat of innocence. It's a cruel taunt every time you glimpse it. You will never know what it's like to empathize. Me, however...I remember a time when I could. And I want—oh, I want badly—to feel it again."

A disgusted look crosses his face. "Well, that is a disappointment."

I tilt my head. "My apologies. I'm sorry I wasted your time."

He shrugs. "You're just confused. I should've done away with the bondage rigger years ago. He's been a distraction that I didn't anticipate. See, I thought I could use him. When I first came to you, you weren't ready for me. So timid. So frightened of your own self. I knew I had to do something to tip the scales." His gaze hardens. "I didn't count on you fucking him."

The cool brush of steel graces my knee. I lift my chin. "We would've found each other regardless. You're not fate's master."

He laughs boldly. "Ah! But look at you now. How you've grown. Look at how strong you've become." He licks his lips. "You've transformed before my eyes, beauty."

"That has nothing to do with you." I let the affront of just who is responsible for my transformation go unsaid. But he knows.

"So, this is our impasse?" he asks.

"I'm afraid so."

The blade slips away again. "I won't accept that. You got off with the man who tortured you. I read your psych evaluations. You were born, Sadie. Admit it. Your abductor uncovered your true nature. He didn't design it."

I push my tumbler farther away, deciding this conversation has gone stale. He's letting his anger slip. "An orgasm is a physiological response to physical stimuli. During rape, it's referred to as an involuntary orgasm. For years—despite what my therapist said—I thought something was wrong with me. If you paid attention to the notes, then you already know that I struggled to become who I am, Price."

"Or struggled to accept what you already were."

Ignoring his baiting comment, I press on. "Colton is the one who helped me accept myself. I don't have to hide who I am with him. No matter how I came to be, he's my answer."

His eyes squint. "So you will accept the weakest explanation. I had higher hopes for you."

I drum my nails on the table. This needs to hurry along.

"I understand why you chose Avery," I say. "Not because you were worried about her discovery of the epithelial cells. No. You planted the evidence to incriminate Simon. You chose her because you had to teach me a lesson. But why Julian?"

He gives me a calculating once over. "You would assume to hurt your dear Colton. But honestly, that was just fun. Blackmailing a blackmailer is always a good time." He sneers. "Seems Julian had a thing for underage girls. It wasn't too hard to pull his strings and get him to hide my presence in the club. That is, until he grew a conscience. But, once the jig was up, he was of no more use."

"You did the honors?"

He chuckles. "No. That sloppy work, along with the lab technician, was all Simon. My eager-to-please apprentice. He was so young. So willing to learn. And so impulsive. Honestly, taking a trophy before you complete the kill? A tooth? How unoriginal. No wonder he suffered from premature ejaculation." He shakes his head. "Alas, as

TRISHA WOLFE

dexterous as I am, I couldn't possibly be everywhere at once. Really, that whipping boy was an unfortunate choice. A convenience that I found and recruited from Connelly's forensic lab." He takes a drink, clears his throat. "But unfortunate choice or not, Simon did come through in the end. I needed—*we* needed—a scapegoat, after all. So that we can start fresh."

The moment of truth. "Why me?"

His eyes beam. "I have so much to learn from you, my love. I had wished to become your apprentice." He exhales an excited, shaky breath. "There can be no greater thrill than to hunt a hunter."

I smile. "And I've truly enjoyed this hunt."

His features fall. "Yes. I suspect you've learned as much from me as I have from you. It's terribly sad that it has to come to an end. I do wish you'd reconsider my offer."

"I'm satisfied where I am."

He sighs dramatically. "Well, disappointment aside, I do have a legacy to carry on."

"Then we're done?"

He chuckles. "Hardly. We've just begun." Dark lust fills his eyes. "We should be leaving now."

"Why would I go anywhere with you?"

"Because—" he sits forward and jabs the point of the blade into my thigh "—I have amassed a collection of evidence on not only your *involvement* with Connelly, but all your other dirty deeds you've committed over the course of your career." He reaches into the inside pocket of his suit and flashes a USB drive before slipping it back in.

"See, I've spent two years studying you, my love. And I came prepared. I was more than happy to let my apprentice take the fall for Connelly, my final gift to you, as it were—but only upon your agreement of my terms."

I shake my head resolutely. "I will never agree."

"Then, you either come with me, or this information finds its way into the hands of your department. I feel confident that you'd rather die than be seen as one of the serial killers you've spent your career hunting." His smile stretches. "See? Preparation. It's of utmost importance."

I nod.

"Move slowly," he says. "I've arranged a lovely homecoming for you. I was so looking forward to it being a celebration in the joining of our talents…but I was also prepared for an alternate ending. Oh, the ending. How I love a good story."

I allow him to lead me out of the bar. He keeps his weapon concealed under his sleeve, his arm stretched across the small of my back. But it's unnecessary. Neither of us will give the other away.

The music of the bar becomes a distant sound the farther we move through the city.

Near the crosswalk, Price turns onto a vacant alley and braces his hand against a building.

"Something wrong?" I ask.

Wiping his brow with the sleeve of his suit, he turns

toward me. "Probably just the excitement of tonight." He attempts a smile, but it's weak. I can see the tremble of his lips.

"Are you sure about that?" I slink closer. "No sudden nausea. Chills. Clammy skin."

He coughs and struggles to suck in a breath. Then, on unsteady feet, staggers down the alley. I follow.

"You should think twice before just *taking what you want*, Price."

He stops. Turns to stare at me, understanding lighting his eyes.

"You can feel your lungs shutting down. The pressure on your chest mimics a heart attack…but it won't be that quick. Or that merciful. You'll appear as docile and calm as if you're simply drifting off to sleep."

He drops to his knees, splays his fingers against the rain-puddled pavement. I crouch beside him. "But the whole time," I continue. "You'll be trapped inside your body. A hostage. Unable to move, to talk—the paralytic fear consuming you."

He wheezes in a tight breath. "What…?"

"Saxitoxin," I answer. "I slipped it into the SoCo. Popular in the sixties as a racy CIA chemical weapon, it was only ever theorized, never put to use. But as you can see, its effectiveness is undeniable."

He stretches out on his back, unconcerned with the Dumpster beside him, the runoff of rancid rainwater staining his suit. "It's so cliché, beauty. Poison?" He coughs around a strained laugh. "You really are venomous."

"Cliché, yes. But you didn't really give me the same courtesy to *prepare* your demise. I had to improvise."

"This is careless," he accuses. "So unlike you. Where will you dispose of me?"

"I've been thinking about that for a while." I walk a circle around him. "But it wasn't until you abducted Avery that the answer presented itself. You didn't think ahead on that one." I *tsk*. "A medical examiner? What if she escaped? Up until the end, you had it all worked out. Simon was supposed to kill Avery and go down for all the murders. All the evidence pointed to him, on his own boat. But what if Avery overpowered him?"

"Impossible. I broke that bitch."

"But you didn't count on us getting to her first." I look down at him. "And here's the kicker: what if once Avery was free, she became the lead M.E. processing your death?"

His eyes widen, the horror of his oversight gripping him as quickly as the toxin.

"For a woman ripe with vengeance—justified vengeance—a shellfish toxin is easily enough explained. I doubt anyone will question Avery's COD report. Especially when your stomach contents will match the menu of the very bar where your credit card was last used."

He clutches his throat, trying to talk. I fill in the gaps for him.

"Too bad you'll be dead and unable to feel Avery slicing open your stomach…filling your bowels with evidence. But just try to picture the smile on her face. Just do it. I'm sure you can recall what she looked like before you stole it from her."

Sometimes, we can be mistaken. I discovered that, once Avery began her recovery, we could talk openly about our newfound connection. There may come a day when her healing journey leads her to a place of remorse for the man who tortured her—but until then, she's bound to secrecy within our world.

With a shaky hand, he beckons me near. One last indulgence, I suppose. I drop down beside him and draw close. "What did you say to him?" he asks, his voice a low rattle. "What did you say to Connelly…there at the end?"

I lean in closer to his ear. "I'm the master."

Yes, I'm the master now. My mentor revealed the killer within—she may have forever lain dormant if not for him. But that was the trigger…*my* trigger. For years, the behaviorist in me tried to dissect it. One in eight abused become the abuser. That's a fact.

I'm the one.

I'm the monster.

Colton once said that I had something taken away from me—but that's not entirely true. My abductor took, but he also gave me the cruel truth of my nature. He unleashed it. He was the catalyst.

Only now, I'm strong enough to resist submitting to it.

A faint smile brushes Price's mouth. Then just as quickly, his eyes no longer see.

I slip on a glove and lift the cuff of his suit. It's a bit overzealous of Price, a bit obvious in his choice. The selection of a sword meant to impress me, but really, it's just a sad extension of his impotent phallus.

Still, the miniature flamberg will look good on my trophy shelf.

At the foot of my bed, I watch the rise and fall of Colton's chest. The moonlight peeks through the slats in the blinds, casting shadows in the room. The alternating light and dark falls across his body, accentuating the dips and arches of his exquisite form.

I push the shoulders of my dress down my arms and step out of my dress. Reaching behind my neck, I undo the clasp of the necklace and then place it and the USB drive in the drawer of my nightstand. Slipping between the cool sheets, I press up against the curve of his back. His body heat warms me instantly, and the harsh chill covering my skin subsides.

I feel the shift in his breathing against my breasts. He stirs, shifting the covers over us as he turns to face me. His warm breath caresses the top of my head, and I tuck myself in the perfectly-designed-for-me nook between his chest and the bed.

"You should've told me," he says, the deep baritone of his voice a low boom in the too-quiet room.

"You would've tried to make me stay," I reply.

"Fuck right."

"Or you would've tried to kill him yourself."

"Absolutely."

I tilt my head back, meeting his dark gaze. "Emotion can't play a part, Colton. That leaves behind a traceable, messy trail."

His hand spreads against my back, the pads of his coarse fingers massaging the muscles along my spine. "Then why take the chance at all."

I release a slow breath. "Because I can't leave him out there as a threat to my mother, or you. Or people I care about like Avery."

"Seems emotion played some part." He roves down to my thigh, bringing my leg over his hip.

I smile into his chest. "That's the irony, I guess."

"How does my dark goddess unwind from a night of hunting?"

Pushing up, I kiss him hard. With passion, and reverence, and the love unfurling within me more and more the longer we're together. I pull back, just enough to whisper, "By commanding her sexy bondage rigger to bind her so tightly, nothing can ever break them apart."

He moves on top of me, his weight pressing me into the mattress, as he reaches for the rope tied to the headboard. "Yes, goddess."

> When you dig deep into the bowels of evil, you cannot hope to reemerge unscathed, unaffected, unchanged—but rather you know without doubt that your character is as fragile and susceptible to fate as the changing tide is to the sea. It's very little to do with choice. And everything to do with risk.

> To her darkness, she whispers. Of monsters and visions of red, of the terrors that claw up from her abyss. Monsters are forged, but heroes are born. To the light, she sings. Of fortitude and acceptance found only in his arms.

> Acceptance is peace.

— SADIE BONDS

Thank you, lovely reader, for taking this dark journey with Sadie and Colton, for reading my words. It means absolutely everything to me. Keep flipping the pages to read a special extended epilogue from Sadie and Colton that I truly hope you enjoy.

Not yet ready to say goodbye to the characters in the *Broken Bonds* world? Start reading **With Ties that Bind** now, featuring Detective Ethan Quinn and medical examiner Avery Johnson as they embark on a new dark and dangerous journey together.

Three Days After Rescue

AVERY

Rocking.

I can still feel the rocking.

I come awake at night to the pitch black—to the void of space and time and consciousness, but always the rocking. As if I'm still trapped in the belly of that boat. Panic grips me so acutely, I thrash and scream until the hospital room comes into focus.

Even then, it's not the reassurance of my surroundings that quiets my hell and stops the screams. I held them in for so long, never giving that monster what he most desired, and now they pour out; a flood channeled through me. Like the dam holding them back cracked with the first one, and my sanity—the mending glue—dissolved under the swell.

But then I feel his hand in mine. That's what brings me back from the brink of madness. I suck in a shuddering breath and let the shiver subside before I look over at him.

Quinn sleeps upright in the chair with his coat bunched up underneath his head. His arm rests on my bed, his hand clutched to mine. My screams never wake him, and I wonder if it's all in my head—if I might still be inside a nightmare that I can't wake from.

He could be a delusion. Some kind of sick dream within the nightmare that offers a glimpse of peace before I'm swallowed by the darkness all over again. Because the screams that blister my throat as they claw up from the sickness…no one could sleep through.

Only he does, and he's been here every night since I shed my first tear, embarrassed that I feared being left alone in the hospital room.

I ease closer to him, lacing my fingers through his. His scent of leather and cologne—so much like a cop—settles over me. I inhale deeply, accepting this moment of peace. Just knowing he's here.

When I'm released tomorrow, what then? When the silence of my own home mocks me and the emptiness consumes my life, how will I cope? I've never feared being alone before.

I don't know how to be a victim.

What's more, I don't want to fear that monster. He's dead. I saw him dead with my own eyes. But there's still this twisting nausea in the pit of my stomach. The darkness whispering that my tormentor lurks everywhere I look. Can a person die of fear? Some nights it feels as if my heart will burst, and I'm tempted to let the panic finally consume me.

Quinn stirs and I release his hand, scared that if he wakes, he'll be the first to let go.

A low knock travels through the room, causing another scream to fire from my lungs. A figure stands in the open doorway, and I know it's Simon… That fucking sick fuck is still alive.

"Avery, it's okay." Sadie enters the room, her voice soft and her face catching the dim glow of the monitor.

"Oh, my God." I press my hand to my chest, shame sweeping over me. "I just... Sometimes it's hard when I first wake up."

"I know," she says. Her gaze shifts from me to Quinn before she settles on the edge of the bed. "I still wake up screaming some nights."

Anger burns lava-red in my vision, my chest aflame. I don't understand whom I'm angry with...or why...but hearing that all this time—all these *years*—hasn't changed anything for Sadie, makes me want to lash out.

"Why are you here?" I ask, the venom thick in my voice. Immediately, regret douses the flames. God, it's a never-ending cycle. "I'm sorry..."

"Don't be." She stands and extends her hand. "You're going to need that anger."

Confusion pushes my brows together, but I accept her hand. "For what?"

With her help, I climb out of the bed, my body—every muscle and bone—sore from the days of torture inflicted on me. As she guides me toward the hallway, I glance back at Quinn.

"He's fine. Can sleep through a hurricane," she assures. "I tried to wake him up once when he fell asleep at his desk"—she shakes her head slowly—"dead to the world."

"Maybe that's why he drew the short straw to be the

one to sit with me." I take a seat on the waiting bench. "He's the only one who can get a full night despite my fits." I try to smile, but the deep cut running through my bottom lip stings from the effort.

Sadie's silence draws my gaze up to her. A serious expression tugs her mouth into a grim line. "Quinn's here on his own. I had no idea," she says.

I look down at my lap, the hospital bracelet circling my wrist. I twirl it, my thoughts muddled. "Then why—?"

"You'll have to ask him." She sits down beside me. "I've come for an entirely different reason. I'm not here to comfort you, Avery. I'm not going to tell you lies about how therapy will help, about how time will heal you. That all you need to do is be strong and fight your demons."

"Damn," I say, a breathy laugh escaping. "Don't sugarcoat it."

"I won't." Her eyes lock with mine; hers unblinking and lit with a surreal gleam that chills me to my bones. "We only discuss this once. From here on out, no matter what you decide, it stays here. Between us."

I should be terrified. This is not the Sadie I know. The woman sitting before me now is cold and methodical, and what she whispers to me in the dark corridor of the hospital should send me fleeing in horror. But as she continues, telling me about a man sitting at a bar, her plan for this man...an eerie calm envelops me, soothing away any trace of fear. Her voice drifts to me, lulling me into a welcome camaraderie, and for the first time since I was plucked from the hellish bowels of The Countess, I feel as if I can take a breath without fearing my own screams.

I make the pact.

It's as simple as slicing open a dead body…which I've done many times over. Then all the fear, the panic, the screams—it all ends. That is the control over my life Sadie grants me in this moment, and I cling to it like a life raft. I crave it so deeply, I'm willing to sell my soul for it.

And so I do.

When I climb back into the hospital bed, I'm no longer the same woman Quinn hauled from that dungeon. I'm not fixed; far from it. But I feel stronger. Only as I go to lay my hand in his…I halt.

Quinn can never know.

Sadie's warning is more than common sense; it's a test.

One that I'm bound to fail if I let myself fall for the detective who's held my hand through the screams and sheltered me from the dark. All done in secrecy, because these are not things done in the light, where we must own to our desires.

So now I have a secret, too. I slip my hand into his large, rough one and curl up next to his strong arm, savoring the feel of his comfort for the last time.

FREE BOOK OFFER

Special gift to Trisha Wolfe readers! Click the link to receive a FREE bonus story featuring your favorite dark romance couple, London and Grayson, from the **Darkly, Madly Duet** .

We weren't born the day we took our first breath. We were born the moment we stole it.

~Grayson Peirce Sullivan, *Born, Darkly*

Meet Grayson Sullivan, AKA The Angel of Maine serial killer, and Dr. London Noble, the psychologist who falls for her patient, as they're drawn into a dark and twisted web. The ultimate cat and mouse game for dark romance lovers. Click here to start the Darkly, Madly Duet now.

EPILOGUE: FOREVER BOUND

COLTON

She's beautiful.

My one, true goddess.

And the fact that she's here, standing so near the center of the rope room right beside me, cements her commitment to us. Just a few short weeks ago as I sat in the seclusion of Sadie's bedroom, fearful...I never imagined that fear would reveal the whole of us.

I didn't believe my own words, not completely, until my goddess returned. Then I knew undoubtedly that we could face anything together. Playing by different rules, embracing our darkest deeds, *is* what's required of our love.

I will never harbor doubt again.

Sadie tugs the collar of her robe more securely around

her neck, then fixes the belt cinching her waist. I can feel her apprehension rolling off her in waves. I lasso the length of rope around my shoulder as I press up against her back.

Tucking my chin in the soft crook of her neck and shoulder, I whisper, "Are you absolutely sure?"

With a deep inhale, she brings my arms around her, resting hers atop mine. "Yes, I'm sure. When I first saw you perform with Katrina…it was like nothing I'd experience before. I envied her. I wanted to be her." She turns to face me in my arms. "This is who you are, Colton. I want to be a part of it. With you."

I grip the silky robe, bunching it in my fist as I snake my other hand down her soft thigh. She trembles slightly against me—and that one action mixed with her devoted confession heightens my need for her. I have half a mind to forget this Shibari session all together and whisk her right back to my room.

But for her, for us—to give her everything she desires and more—I commit fully to this session. I haven't performed publicly since the first time I bound Sadie in my ropes. I haven't needed to. The drive I once felt to be free of my guilt no longer tortures me. But I still love the thrill of it. Feeling the awe from the crowd when they experience the pure passion through the model's rapture.

It's the one thing I was able to give Marni when her pain became too much. And when it was no longer enough, when the pain was unbearable and she couldn't disappear into her subspace, my abyss consumed me.

Every session I performed from then on was an attempt to correct that failure within myself. To banish her fear and pain… With every band of rope, with every cinch of the knots, I desperately needed to feel the other person's relief —to make it my own.

Until Sadie.

The moment I performed for her and saw that raw longing in her jewel green eyes, I knew I would never need to seek that acceptance in another again. And I was right. She fulfills that bottomless abyss within me, just as I tether her to a safe world where she doesn't loathe who she truly is.

With restrained want, I release the robe and drag my hands up her body until I reach her shoulders. Slipping my hand inside the robe, I run my thumb over the scar along her collarbone. "You're more than a part of me, goddess. You're the greatest part—the ultimate part that completes me." I taste her lips then. Unable to deny myself this indulgence, I caress her mouth slowly, tenderly, stoking the never-ending inferno inside me.

Around us, sultry music bleeds into a steady drumbeat. Bass fills the room, transitioning into a symphony of violins. The volume builds and builds, until I can discern the intro to Barber's *Adagio For Strings*. The piece I painstakingly searched and selected for her—a piece that conveys this crucial moment between Sadie and I. It wasn't an easy task, as so much of my collection I can now hear and visualize Sadie in the music. But this piece…I wanted something dark, and haunting, yet transitions into the purity that we found in each other.

As the melody pulls me under, I'm almost lost to the kiss—more than tempted to steal Sadie away this instant. I forcefully pull back and release a heavy breath. "Follow me."

She laces her fingers through mine as I lead her toward the middle of the rope room. There's no stage here, but the intense feeling of being on display is almost more pronounced. As if on cue, the music swells as club members form a circle around us. Curtains are pulled back at the booths for a clear view.

I know this is the part Sadie dreads. She's hidden in the shadows for so long, frightened of her own nature, erecting a barrier between herself and the world. Lowering her walls leaves her feeling vulnerable, but she is not weak. The scar marring her chest is not proof of her limitations or defect; it is proof of her strength.

And as I remove her robe, sliding the sleeves down to reveal that scar to the world, I lift my chin, encouraging Sadie to own her very visceral power. The robe pools to the floor around her bare feet, and she stands before me, a beautiful, radiant goddess illuminated by the spotlight. Her creamy skin is luminescent, blending with her nude, strapless bra and underwear.

It was at my request she adorn this attire. There is

nothing shameful about her body, or any other naked form, but Sadie's body belongs to *me*. I may not mind sharing our sessions, in order to help bring Sadie to this next level...but the intimacy we share, her body and mine, belongs solely to us.

I move in close and capture her waist. "The crowd is hidden by the dark, goddess. And there is no judgment here. Remember how you felt when you first witnessed a session." I press my lips to her forehead. "You're gifting them something amazing."

Gently, her hands seek my chest as she places her palms over my heart. "I'm ready."

With her permission, I raise one hand and direct the rope to descend. The silver ring glints in the beam of light as it lowers toward us. I remove the rope from my shoulder and methodically tie one end to the ring, preparing the stage.

I've done this many times before, always knowing that I myself was never the center. My actions were a spectacle, a performance; it was the model's experience that became the focus. Now, understanding this, it feels as if I'm offering up my whole world—inviting others to kneel before my goddess as I elevate her on a pedestal.

That's where she belongs, of course. But I won't lie to myself, pretending that I'm not affected. Jealousy lives inside me, chaste and heady, wishing I could keep this lovely creature all to myself. Only I know that is wrong. To lock her away is a crime. Her captor did just that.

Wells attempted the same. Their sin will not become my own.

With the last of my conviction, I band the main strand of rope around Sadie's chest, working the coarse rings up around her torso. I let the rope slide and flow through my palms as I loop her harness, fastening tightly woven knots along her back.

"You're strong, Sadie," I whisper to her. "You're my vision. You were my vision before I ever laid eyes on you." I've never worked with a more patient model before. It's as if Sadie disappears somewhere between reality and her subspace during the preparation. She finds a pocket of her own world where she pulls from, and though I'm assured I'm there with her, this is her strength alone.

I tighten the harness just a notch, hearing the ropes creak above the music—a seamless merger of beauty and pain, a masterful orchestra. The harmony sends chills down my back as I take in Sadie's smooth skin rippling with this same effect. Then I kneel before her and uncoil a new rope—deep red, the color of passion, lust. Craving.

I brace my back, my knees digging into the hardwood floor, as I lace her ankles. The friction of the rope nearly sends me over the edge as I wind it around her slender calves. And the contrast—the beautiful contrast of the red against her porcelain skin—pangs my chest. I want so badly to mount a spreader bar between her legs and take her into my mouth, make her tremble with the raw need attacking me right now.

And here is the blurred line. The reason why I never mixed pleasure and work before. This is as much a test of my endurance with this new arrangement as it is for Sadie. The crowd falls away, disappearing with the swell of music, and I only feel and see her. I'm lost to this woman. Bound and destined to serve her.

This testament of my devotion pours from me as I continue to weave an intricate pattern up her leg, my fingers taking every advantage to probe and caress her silky skin along the way. As the music lowers, sweeping an awed hush through the room, I can feel the ecstasy of the many people hungrily devouring our scene.

I can sense their envy. Taste their yearning. Hear their gasps of desire. Wishing they, too, could obtain this pureness of connection we've mastered between us. That brings me back to my work. Our passion is reserved for us. Although I'm allowing them a glimpse, I can't be lost completely to the moment.

Standing, I reach up and tie off the end of the rope to the ring, bringing Sadie's feet off the floor. Her body molds to the shape of the harness, a canopy of ropes suspending her torso and limbs to form a perfect arc.

Our eyes meet as I lower my face before hers. "Take me there, Colton," she says. "I'm yours. All yours. Only you can touch me."

I suck in a sharp breath, my teeth clamp down hard at her vow. Palming her cheek, I swipe my thumb beneath her eye, clearing away the perspiration glistening there under the heated spotlight.

My fingers curl toward my palms as I grip my hands into fists, reining in my desire. Control has never been so impossible. Especially when we're about to embark on a new experience. As soon as we end this session...Sadie's mine.

SADIE

The restraint Colton is exuding to keep his emotions in check shows clearly in the rigid lines of his face. This is a performance, yes, but it's also so much more—a window to the sanctity between us.

During our first session, he kept himself blank, expressionless. Which I believe he did so for my sake, so that my focus was internal—on myself and my experience —rather than fearing anything from the man restraining me.

For this, I respect his professionalism. He was able to give me what I needed then, and even more of what I didn't even realize I craved and desired as we advanced.

I've watched him perform. I've seen his muscles working, gathering and straining as he finessed the rope, his focus masterful as he constructed elaborate shapes and designs with his model.

It's empowering to witness—just to preview his soulful, erotic creations. Because, ultimately, that's what he is; an artist. And yet, between us, even before this very crowd, our connection strips him of that shield. I broke through his armor just as absolutely as he shredded mine. Our link is impossible to curb before these watchful eyes.

As the ropes tighten, cradling me securely, he anchors the main line and pulls me farther away from the floor. As I'm lifted, I can almost forget about the audience—my subspace calling me home, my love for Colton deflecting any fear of the unknown. It's because of this trust that I was able to commit to the session. When Colton told me that he was no longer going to perform publicly for The Lair, I knew it was wrong. I couldn't allow that.

Watching him that first night was my initial step toward acceptance. In finding and discovering myself. It would be shameful to deny that to another soul. What he offers—though maybe first demonstrated through his own pain and suffering—is a gift. He shouldn't feel obligated to deny anyone his talent because of his devotion to me.

I've since come to fully understand his desire of goddess worship. And I take that role in our relationship seriously. At any point, I could've allowed jealousy and my own insecurities to command him not to perform, keeping him all to myself. It was tempting. But I knew just as surely that I *should* command him to perform Shibari.

I was the pivotal piece in the game that had to change.

Offering myself willingly and freely to his audience, so that his talent can be experienced, was my own selfless act. My gift to him.

And seeing him perform now, his limber movements graceful, his expert hands sure, I'm certain in our roles. He is my dominant, just as I am his goddess. It is equal give and take between us.

The music begins to build again, and though I can't see it, I can feel the climax to the performance nearing. Colton's gaze captures something beyond me, and a slight hesitancy worms into my stomach. A sickness, a dread. It's the same fear I encountered when my captor prepared me for the cross.

More so than the instrument he used to break me...the cane that attacked my body...the St. Andrew's cross instilled me with a shameful loathing that scorched my humanity. Stretched out and open, bared and unable to shield my flesh, it was the spark that awakened the demon within.

Colton was hesitant, worried that tapping into this fear before others would be a setback rather than a liberation. And I do understand his reasoning. As a behaviorist, I would never dare instruct another to attempt something so threatening to their psyche. Mine has already been shattered once, my mind splintered. Forcing me to adopt an antisocial persona in order to protect the other, vulnerable half.

My own personal defense mechanism.

But the truth is, Colton's love freed that necessary evil when he caned me. Something so monumental between us couldn't possibly be outshone. In private, strapping me to the cross would be erotic, sensual, beautiful—because my trust and love for him has already been established. There are no more barriers to deconstruct. The shame the cross still harbors for me must be conquered by what it ultimately stands for: humiliation.

My captor put me on display when he chained me to his cross. So I knew, within the deepest, darkest corner of my mind, Colton's sessions and my fears were to be tied together. It's the reason we found each other. Why we balance each other so completely.

It was the inevitable next step in our relationship.

I force my chin higher, keeping my eyes open and making myself aware of the crowd, holding my subspace at bay as the cross comes into my line of sight. A trickle of humiliation creeps over me—but just as quickly, Colton is there, his rough palm against my back. Offering me his strength.

Then I see it. Those standing around to form a circle, in their eyes, their expressions. *Understanding.* This is more than an erotic fantasy for them. They do not view me as deviant, or misunderstood. They empathize with the knowledge that we may understand ourselves better than most. This is our dark world where we bare our souls, seeking enlightenment.

The cross is spun around by two members as part of the presentation, and it's beautiful. Crafted by Colton himself, love and devotion went into its making. The wood is of the deepest red oak, the silver rope hooks gleam, and a wide base supports the elegant structure.

Colton stands beside the cross, his vibrant blue eyes hard on me, waiting for my consent. And I don't hesitate. I speak loud and clear for the whole room. "I'm captive to you."

His eyes close for a brief moment, allowing me to witness the quake roll through his body. Then with devastatingly gorgeous movements, his jeans riding low on his hips, chest bare and glistening in the light, he reaches for the rope and hauls me alongside the cross.

With the production in mind, he spins me full circle, showcasing the graceful Shibari design wrapping my body. He then guides me before the cross and begins to rig it. Each rope that cradles me is released, one by one, as he threads them through the hooks. It's a slow and sensual process as I seamlessly transition through each position. First my legs, posed with one knee bent, the other extended, as he loosens the harness and rights me with my back to the crossed boards.

My breaths come faster as the constriction surrounding my torso loosens, and I feel the cool brush of the wood against my skin. The sudden rush of air ignites a weightlessness, thrilling and euphoric. And when Colton unthreads my legs and drops down before me to tie my ankles to the cross, I feel the pull—my body commanding my mind to slip.

I don't hold off any longer. I allow the calming

awareness of my subspace to take over as Colton guides me there. The classical harmony envelops me, twining and merging with the ropes lacing my wrists, my stomach and chest. With my arms extended outward, my legs spread, I should feel exposed, helpless. But it's the most empowering feeling I've ever experienced.

Then Colton's lips are on mine, drinking in my release of fear and pain, and filling me in return, emboldening me. This wasn't a planned part of the scene—it's a burning hunger, a thirst that must be quenched. It's the part of us that demands to be answered with each other.

I will never belong to my captor again. I will never succumb to the command of my demons. I will never fear who I am. Bound and breathless, in Colton's ropes, his sweet taste of redemption on my lips, I am whole.

And just as surely as we are bound, we are free.

My arms ache. The thin rope linking my wrists tightens, biting into my skin, as the weight of my dangling body submits to gravity. My flushed skin tingles where the flogger strikes. Each time the leather tails make contact, Colton groans, making my thighs slick with wetness.

I couldn't possibly heighten this moment between us any more, our desire already cresting beyond the breaking point, but I'd be remiss not to try. "You wanted to fuck me," I breathe out. "Right there, in front of all of them. Show them who makes me come, over and over. Who owns this body."

His deep growl rumbles through the private chamber, and the flogger stings my ass. Then his knee is there, pressing against my stomach, tilting my backside up toward him as he towers over me. He brings the flogger down, sending the tails against my core. I buck, needing to reposition myself, as I grind against his thigh, seeking stimulation for my clit.

"I'm beyond suffering, goddess," Colton says, the restrain heavy in his deep voice. "End it. Give me permission to prove how badly I wanted that right now. Let me fuck you hard and raw…"

"Not yet," I command. "I want you shaking with need first."

Removing his knee, he releases me and drops down before my suspended body. The sight of his erection—so hard and seeking—scorches my insides with a fiery ache, the throb between my legs making me quiver. But I know I have to prolong it…bring my Dom to the edge—for his pleasure and mine.

Untethering my ankles, he brings one of my legs up over his shoulder. With unguarded desire, he sinks his teeth into the flesh of my thigh, eliciting a cry from my mouth.

"Yes, goddess. I'm yours to break." His mouth

hungrily roams up my thigh, his tongue massaging each piercing nip his teeth deliver.

A whimper escapes, and I'm suddenly undulating my hips closer, demanding his mouth to take me. He always anticipates what I crave, and he's there, his hot tongue forceful as he tastes me, spreading my lips and sucking me into his mouth. A yearning pulls at my back. I arch against the restraint, unable to control my labored breathing.

It's divine agony. The throb blooms into a needy ache that demands pressure. And he knows this, too. His tongue flicks my clit, bringing me so close...but not giving me nearly enough.

My heels dig into his strong back as I squirm, desperate for penetration. He only clasps my hips, forcing me to still as he takes his time, drawing out the pleasure. His fingers grip me hard, and I feel him tense beneath me, needing release.

I'm beyond there—my head thrown back as I gasp for a cool breath to sate the burn devouring my lungs. I look down. "Stroke your cock," I order.

His teeth nip my clit as he shudders, but he obeys. Pushing away, Colton heaves a strenuous breath as he takes himself in his hand. My breasts pang, my nipples pebbled and ready to have equal attention, as I watch him stroke his shaft. All the way to the base, then slowly toward the head. The tip glistens, giving away how close he is to breaking.

"Stop," I say, and his hand halts. "Push inside me...

hard and fast…and stay there. Until I demand to be fucked."

He pushes to his knees and grabs my waist, then sweeps me forward. Anchoring his forearms beneath my legs, he slams into my hot ache in one, quick motion, causing me to cry out.

As he pulses inside me, rock-hard, my walls clamp down around him. The yearning in my back travels through my whole body, and I flinch, unable to suppress my desire. At this slight movement, I feel myself soak his hard length.

Colton grits his teeth as his eyes bore into me. And the need to be fulfilled overrides all logic.

"Fuck me, Colton. Don't hold back."

With a groan, he wraps an arm around my back and hauls me closer, his chest giving my nipples the friction they crave, as he drives into me with more force. He buries his mouth in my neck, his teeth sinking into my skin as he finds purchase to ram his cock into me over and over… each time deeper and more claiming than the last.

"Goddess…" His desperate plea, my name on his lips, sends me spiraling toward my climax.

"I'm yours. Fucking take me," I plead. No longer able to command, I adopt my submissive place beneath him. I need him just as desperately to control me—to dominate my orgasm.

He releases a guttural roar as he quickens his pace, his hard want taking and claiming, slamming into me with unguarded vigor. "Fuck... You're so fucking perfect," he whispers against my skin. "Come, goddess. I need to feel you come."

I tremble against the restraint, my arms stretched and pulling at the ropes as his momentum intensifies, driving me over the edge. I break all at once. Completely and utterly, with his arms anchoring me close, his chest my solid wall of support.

"That's fucking right." He smacks my ass hard, ratcheting up my orgasm as it rolls through me. Then with a fast jerk, he pulls out and flips me around, positioning my back up against his chest.

He uses his knees to spread my legs wide as he places his cock at the entrance of my channel. Bracing his hand over my mouth, he says, "Bite down." Then, gently but powerfully, he pushes into me fully. The immediate sensation of pain mixing with pleasure draws out a long moan. As his thickness opens me to take him, the friction of his hard length presses against my walls...and I react. My teeth bear down on his hand.

A severe curse, then he expels a sharp hiss as I flex, tightening around him. He thrusts deeper. "Goddess...hell. I'm already fucking there with you."

I kick my ass out, giving him better access, loving the sound of his deep and needy groans. He grabs my breasts, his fingers splaying over them and pinching my nipples, causing my belly and every muscle in my body to tense.

"Oh, goddess...fuck." He pumps hard into me once

more and shatters. As his hips continue to rock, he fills me, and the feel of him spilling down my thighs makes me quiver and sag against the rope.

He reaches up and tugs the lead rope, releasing the restraint. I fall against him as his strong arms cradle me close, his hot breath searing and tender along my neck. His grip tightens as the last of his orgasm spirals out, and I cling to his arms, lost within his embrace.

"I'm yours," he whispers into my hair, the scruff of his chin sending a shiver over my skin as he presses a kiss to my shoulder. "Forever bound to you, goddess."

Rapture never felt this perfect. This sublime. But that's what it is; the only word that feels right in this moment. "Forever," I whisper.

Start reading the next chapter in the Broken Bonds series in With Ties that Bind now.

TRISHA WOLFE READING ORDER

All Trisha's series are written to read on their own and pull you in, but here is her preferred reading order to introduce worlds and characters that cross over in each series.

Broken Bonds Series

With Visions of Red

With Ties that Bind

Derision

Darkly, Madly Duet

Born, Darkly

Born, Madly

A Necrosis of the Mind Duet

Cruel

Malady

Hollow's Row Series

Lovely Bad Things

Lovely Violent Things

Lovely Wicked Things

Dark Mafia Romance

Marriage & Malice

Devil in Ruin

Standalone Novels

Marrow (co-written)

Lotus Effect

Cellar Door

Five of Cups

ABOUT TRISHA WOLFE

From an early age, Trisha Wolfe dreamed up fictional worlds and characters and was accused of talking to herself. Today, she lives in South Carolina with her family and writes full time, using her fictional worlds as an excuse to continue talking to herself. Get updates on future releases at TrishaWolfe.com

Want to be the first to hear about new book releases, special promotions, and signing events for all Trisha Wolfe books? Sign up for Trisha Wolfe's VIP list

Connect with Trisha Wolfe on social media on these platforms: Facebook | Instagram | TikTok

Made in the USA
Columbia, SC
15 January 2025